The Manatee Girl

by

Doris Wheelus

Bloomington, IN Milton Keynes, UK

authorHOUSE®

AuthorHouse™
1663 Liberty Drive, Suite 200
Bloomington, IN 47403
www.authorhouse.com
Phone: 1-800-839-8640

AuthorHouse™ UK Ltd.
500 Avebury Boulevard
Central Milton Keynes, MK9 2BE
www.authorhouse.co.uk
Phone: 08001974150

First published by AuthorHouse 1/11/2007

ISBN: 978-1-4259-6689-8 (sc)

Printed in the United States of America
Bloomington, Indiana

This book is printed on acid-free paper.

Dedication

This book is dedicated to my husband, Roger Wheelus, my daughter, Pam Jones and my grandchildren, Mandy & Tyler Cook, Joshua Hinton, and Summer Jones. Also to my great-grandchildren, Braden, Teagon, and Maybree Cook. Thanks also to my writing class at TCC and my writing friends, Joe Palmer, Anna Myers, Suzan King, Jane Mills, Mary Shackelford, Diane Moore, Nita Buckley, Faye Holmes, Inge Kahn, Jean Connely and June Box. For Alice Duncan who wouldn't let me give up. For my emotional cheerleaders, Joyce Bremec and the late Lennie Rodgers who prayed daily for my writing.

Thanks to Editor, Philip Martin for his years of encouragement and belief in this book. A special thank you to a great lady, Janet Volkman. Thanks to Gardner Wood for his help with research. Appreciate all the help from Nancy Sadusky, Christine Strickland and the Save the Manatee Club. Your dedication to these gentle giants has kept them alive.

Especially for my Great Niece, Diana DeGarmo, who fought valiantly and beat the cancer and who named herself

Clarice for this book. This is for her brilliant grandfather, Clarence DeGarmo, who proofed my manuscripts with care and knowledge.

Most of all I dedicate this book to the Manatee Girl who inspired me to write this story to help save the manatees. I didn't get your name at the canals behind the power plant in Vero Beach. You were about 12. You taught me to love those manatees. They were so special that I spent eight years on this book so our beloved manatees would become important to others. My wish is that this book will make a difference and that we will meet again one day.

Acknowledgments

For my Beautiful Cherokee People.

Chapter One

"In Oklahoma it's cold enough to freeze the horns off a bull," Mandy said. "It isn't fair. Here in Florida, it's like summertime."

Crosslin grinned.

Mandy looked at the Seminole Indian boy. She liked the way he looked in his baggy jean shorts cut off just below his knees. His gray shirt hung loosely from his broad shoulders to his hips. "You're shy, aren't you?" she said.

"A little," Crosslin said quietly and looked away.

"My daddy was shy. You remind me of him. He was Native American, too. I sure miss him."

Crosslin looked at Mandy. His eyes softened. "Your grandmother told us he died."

This kid has feelings. Mandy liked that. She waited for him to say more, and he didn't. "You don't talk much, do you? My grandmothers says I'm a talker." She stretched out her arms and spun around twice. She couldn't believe she had just said that. She wasn't a talker at all. In fact, she was a bookworm and the quietest girl in her homeroom class.

Crosslin had a slight grin on his face. He looked down.

Mandy grinned. She hoped that whopper didn't get back to Nana. She looked at Crosslin. "It's good getting away from home. I can't believe I'm in sunny Florida on spring break." She spun around again. "I love it here."

Crosslin stopped walking and stood in the middle of the sidewalk. "I love it, too. I was glad your grandmother asked me to walk you to the canals to see the manatees. It's good to get away from my sister. She drives me nuts."

"I know what you mean. Sisters can be like that. My little four-year-old sister drives me up the wall. After Daddy died, my mama had to go to work. I take care of her a lot. She won't mind me at all. I think that's why I was glad to get the letter from Nana."

Crosslin looked puzzled. "Nana? Who's Nana?" Crosslin asked

"Your next door neighbor. My grandmother. I call her Nana."

"I call my grandmother, Grandma," Crosslin said.

Mandy felt relieved Crosslin hadn't asked about her daddy's death. He wasn't nosey like most kids. Mandy liked his looks, too. Crosslin was a cutie. He wore his long straight hair pulled back into a braid. It was black as a raven's wing. Dare she tell Crosslin the truth? No, that was one secret she must keep. Who would want to be her friend if they knew she had caused her own father's death?

Mandy's hair was as long as Crosslin's but not quite as dark. Her hair was more brown than black, and she had it pulled up in a high ponytail. She was Cherokee Indian from her dad's side, but it was something that was never discussed. Anytime her dad had tried to talk to her about being Native American, her mother would interrupt their conversation.

As they walked to the canals behind the power plant, Mandy told Crosslin how she had e-mailed her grandmother here in Vero Beach to ask her to find some stick-on-stars she could put on her ceiling. Her mother had called around Tulsa but couldn't find a store that carried them.

When the envelope came from her Florida grandmother, Mandy was a little confused. There were no stars in the envelope but instead an airline ticket to come to Vero Beach for spring break. A note read, "Come and we'll shop for those stars together."

As she held the airline tickets she realized it was up to her mother. "Please Mother, please. Let me go. It will be heaven being in sunny Florida. I'm sick of cold weather."

Her mother had looked worried. "It's so far. You'll have to change planes."

"My friend flew to his grandmother, and the airline people helped him change planes. You can arrange it ahead of time. Please, Mother. Please."

Her mother had finally said yes. Mandy grabbed her mother and hugged her so hard her mother squealed. Mandy packed her suitcase that night. It was another week before she could leave, but she wanted to be ready. Every morning she woke up smiling. Some days at school, she felt so excited she could barely stay in her seat.

When she had dressed to leave she put her bathing suit on first and put her clothes over it. She wanted to be ready just in case they stopped at the ocean first.

Mandy told Crosslin about her flight from Tulsa. She had been nervous about flying alone. The airline people helped her change planes in Atlanta. When she got on the second plane, she worried she might not remember her grandmother. Her heart pounded. When she got off the plane, there was Nana waving both arms above her head. When Mandy walked into her grandmother's pillow-soft body, she remembered the smell of her honeysuckle talcum powder. She knew she was safe.

Mandy looked at Crosslin. "The weather here is heavenly." She glanced down the street. "Race you to that telephone pole."

Crosslin sprinted ahead of Mandy and grinned as he slapped the telephone pole first.

Mandy looked at the Indian boy. She was surprised he could outrun her. "You're fast. Do you run track?"

Crosslin shook his head. "No, we don't have a track coach in elementary. Next year I'll be in junior high. I'll run then. Do you run track?"

"Yeah, I do. I run on a team called the Wind Chasers. We have lots of fun. I'll be in seventh grade next term. We're about the same age." Mandy took a deep breath. "What's that smell?" She took another deep breath to fill her lungs with the delicate, sweet smell. "I love it."

Crosslin grinned. "Isn't it great? The wind is carrying the scent of the orange blossoms from the groves. My grandfather said it's a gift from the wind."

Mandy smiled, "He's right. It is a gift. Let's hurry. I want to see a manatee. Race you to the fence." Mandy reached the fence first and bounced against the chain links. After scanning the water several minutes, she sighed in frustration. "Where are they?"

Crosslin gazed out at the water. "The manatees usually surface every five minutes, but they can hold their breath up to 20 minutes. Look for circles in the water. You'll see their backs come up first,"

Mandy shivered with excitement. "I've never seen one up close," she said.

"It's great to see them. Not many people get to see them unless they go to Sea World in Orlando or a few special places. Sea World takes care of the injured ones."

Mandy frowned. "Injured? How do they get injured?"

"People in boats," Crosslin said. A flash of hot anger crossed his face. He looked at the ground. "The manatees move slowly. Stupid people, who don't watch, run into them and their boat propellers cut deeply into the manatees' backs and sides. Many of the manatees die."

"Die? Because of boats?" Mandy asked.

"Yes. Either the boat hits them and kills them instantly or the wounds from the propeller cuts get infected, and they die later. We have a chart on our bulletin board at school. The boaters killed 80 in 2005 by not slowing down," Crosslin said. "The paper said a total of 396 manatees died in 2005."

"That's terrible," Mandy said. "Maybe it'll get better."

"I don't think so," Crosslin said.

"Why not?" Mandy asked.

"Each year it gets worse. People aren't careful, and many don't care. The boaters killed as many manatees in the first two months of 2005 as they usually do all year," Crosslin said.

Mandy curled her fingers around the chain links. "How many are left?" Mandy asked.

"Not many. No one knows for sure. If the winter is cold they die from the cold water," Crosslin said.

"Maybe the new babies will make up for the ones they killed," Mandy said as she let go of the fencing and turned to face Crosslin.

Crosslin shook his head. Mandy couldn't believe how sad his eyes looked. "Not so," he said. "A female manatee doesn't have a calf every year. It's usually every three to five years. They're killing the manatees so fast they're going to be gone soon."

Mandy could feel the heat of anger travel up to her face. How could people not care? This was serious business to Crosslin, and it was becoming important to her, too. "Does it take a manatee three to five years to have a baby?" she asked.

Crosslin looked out at the water. He looked back at Mandy and shook his head. "No. It takes 12 to 13 months, but they keep their calf with them for almost two years, and I guess they don't usually have another until that one is grown and on its own."

Mandy's eyes searched the water. "Where are those manatees? I want to see one right now."

Crosslin chuckled. "Be patient. They do what they want. We aren't able to call them. No one can do that but Jill, the Manatee Girl." When the manatees didn't surface, Crosslin said, "Do you mind if we rest a little?" He pointed to a nearby shade tree. "I got up at 4 a.m. to throw my friend's paper route and I'm wasted."

They walked to a nearby oak tree. Crosslin sat down, then leaned his back against the tree. Mandy dropped down next to him. They were silent. Mandy knew Crosslin was tired when he stretched out and used his arm for a pillow.

Crosslin was soon snoring.

Mandy closed her eyes, but it was always the same. The memory. "Daddy," she whispered to herself, "I'm so sorry. Please forgive me." She put her head on her knees. When she heard crying, she thought it was her own, but it wasn't.

When she glanced toward the water, she saw the most beautiful girl. Her long blonde hair hung down her back like a fairy princess. She looked to be about twelve.

The girl cried as she leaned toward the water. Why? Her voice was musical even as she sobbed.

What was she doing and why was she crying? This girl didn't cry an ugly cry. This girl cried pretty. "Crosslin, wake up," Mandy said.

"No," he mumbled.

She shoved his shoulder. "Come on, Crosslin. There's a girl by the water. I think it's the Manatee Girl. Get up."

"Too tired," Crosslin whispered.

"Okay," Mandy said as she hurried to the girl's side and sat on the ground next to her. "Hi," she said.

"Hi," the girl replied.

"Are you Jill, the Manatee Girl?"

The girl looked at Mandy and nodded. She looked puzzled. "How do you know my name?"

"Crosslin talks about you. He calls you the Manatee Girl."

"Really? He's nice. He loves the manatees, too," Jill said.

"He was hoping you'd be here so you could call the manatees. He stretched out under that tree to rest, and now he's really sawing logs."

Jill laughed. "He must have thrown Billy's paper route. Right?"

Mandy laughed. "Yeah. How did you know?"

"He told me the other day that Billy was trying to get him to throw the route, so he could go out of town with his parents."

"I'd hate to get up at 4 a.m.," Mandy said.

"Me, too," the Manatee Girl said. "I'd never make it."

Mandy looked at the pretty girl and smiled. "I heard you crying. Are you okay?"

The girl nodded. "Yeah, I'm okay. Are you okay? I heard you crying, too."

Mandy nodded. "Yeah, I cry a lot. My dad died last year."

The Manatee Girl wiped her eyes. "It's hard when you love someone, and they die."

Mandy looked away. "It's harder when it's your fault they died."

Jill looked shocked. "What makes you say that?"

Mandy felt that choking lump fill her throat. She couldn't believe she was telling this girl things, secret things that only she and her mother knew.

Somehow, it felt good to share it. She could almost hear a voice say, "Tell it. Let it out." She took a deep breath. "Every Tuesday evening my dad and I ran on the high school track. One Tuesday I didn't want to run because Mom rented me a new video game that just came out. It was my reward for being picked Student of the Month. I wanted to brag at school that I had already played the new game, so I didn't go running with my dad."

A look of pain crossed Mandy's face. "Well, Daddy never came home so we drove to the school to look for him. We found him dead on the high school track. He had a heart attack, and no one was around to call 911. If I had gone with him, he wouldn't have died. I killed him."

"How awful," Jill said.

"It's been the worst year of my life," Mandy said. She looked at the pretty girl. "Why were you crying? Were you crying about the manatees?"

Jill shook her head. "No, family problems. Sort of like yours but not quite as bad."

"Want to talk about it?" Mandy asked.

"No, it's just too awful to talk about. Maybe later," Jill said.

Mandy liked this girl, and she knew if she wanted to be her friend she better talk about something else. "Isn't it beautiful here? The grass is so green, and the flowers are blooming. Our grass in Oklahoma is still brown. This place is heavenly. Especially the weather."

Jill laughed. "You ought to be here in July. You can fry an egg on the sidewalk."

Mandy shrugged. "Oh, that's no big deal. You can do that in July in Oklahoma, too. I need to go back to my Nana's to get something to feed the manatees."

"No!" the Manatee girl's voice stopped Mandy. "You can't do that!"

Mandy turned to face Jill. She was confused and hurt by the girl's tone. It was as if she were angry with her. She hadn't done anything. What was wrong? "Why not?" she asked, puzzled and curious.

"It's dangerous for the animals. They feed off sea grasses and underwater plants. Other things can kill them."

"Really?" Mandy moved closer to her, interested.

"Yeah, people hand-fed this one little baby manatee palm fronds."

"What's that?" Mandy asked.

"It's the leafy branches from a palm tree. The people thought they were helping, but the palm fronds stopped up his intestinal tract and the little manatee died," Jill said.

"How awful," Mandy said. "Those people thought they were helping, but they weren't."

"I know. They didn't mean to hurt him, but it happened. There's another reason not to feed them. Crosslin's grandfather said if people fed them they could get lazy and might not teach their young how to feed on vegetation in the water. He said if you feed them they will feel safe around people and head for people in the boats and get cut by the boat propellers."

"Does that happen a lot?" Mandy asked.

"It does. The wildlife people are trying hard to help them. They have a big sign down behind the power plant which says if you feed them you can be fined for harassment."

"Boy, if someone was feeding me I wouldn't consider it harassment. Would you?" Mandy asked.

"No, but the wildlife people know what they're doing."

"That's good. Someone needs to help the manatees. We came so I could see the manatees, but they wouldn't come up for us," Mandy said. She watched Jill brush her long silky blonde hair from her face. The Manatee Girl's blue eyes were such a bright blue, Mandy wondered if she wore blue contacts. Her eyes were different and seemed to glow.

"Do you want me to call them?" the Manatee Girl asked.

"Yes. Oh yes," Mandy pleaded.

Mandy's own hair and eyes were brown. How she longed to have blonde hair and blue eyes like the Manatee Girl.

"Let me get down on that rock ledge near the water," Jill said. "I need to snap off a twig of crepe myrtle to signal them to come."

Jill walked carefully down the bank.

Mandy nodded and followed her down the bank to the flat rock.

Jill smiled.

Mandy thought Jill was the prettiest girl she had ever seen.

"This is where Crosslin and I call the manatees. I thought you both were asleep until I heard you crying," the Manatee Girl said.

Mandy smiled. "We were waiting for you. I've never seen a manatee up close."

Jill looked out at the water. "They're so special. There's no other animal like them." Jill brushed the dried leaves, dirt and twigs from the flat rock ledge. A large low limb from a crepe myrtle provided shade. Mandy was surprised the crepe myrtle was more like a tree than a bush. They huddled close as the young girl began to swish the twig back and forth into the water.

Jill stared at Mandy. "The manatees are my friends. I can't put them in danger. They're slow moving and bad people have hurt them in the past."

"I understand. I won't hurt them," Mandy said.

Jill nodded. "I believe you. When you see Tubs, you'll understand."

Mandy watched the intense look on the young girl's face as she concentrated on getting the manatees to surface. It was as if she were hypnotized as she stared into the water and stirred the small crepe myrtle sprig back and forth.

Almost instantly, three large gray faces rose from the water. "Whoa!" Mandy felt her heart pound. She could not believe what she was seeing. She felt as if she were in a dream. Each manatee held its face above the water for Jill to stroke. Mandy now knew why Crosslin called Jill the Manatee Girl.

"Look," Jill said and pointed. "Marie has her new baby with her. She wants us to see it."

Mandy looked down to see where Jill was pointing.

"The baby is called a calf. See how it stays close to its mother? I call the baby manatee Tiny Tina."

Mandy looked down at the manatees lined up next to the bank. She pointed. "The mother is Marie and her calf is Tiny Tina. Right?"

"Right," Jill said. "Next to Marie is Brutus. You can rub their faces gently. They like it."

Mandy reached for Marie. As she lightly stroked the manatee's face, she felt as if she were in a dream. The manatee's skin reminded her of the elephant she had once touched at a carnival. When she touched the nose, she was surprised. It felt like velvet. She was surprised to feel stiff whiskers on the manatee's upper lip. She knew this would be a moment she would remember all her life. "Will the baby let me touch her?"

"Probably. Marie will tell her there is no danger."

Mandy laughed. "The baby doesn't look very tiny to me. How big will it get?"

"Well, the calf is probably around 60 pounds now, and she could get over 3,000 pounds when she's grown." Jill pointed, "Oh look, here comes the biggest manatee. I call him Tubs because he is the largest and probably the oldest. I'm sure he is over 3,000 pounds. When he comes up, notice his back."

When Tubs' back appeared above the water, Mandy gasped. Carved into the manatee's back in block letters were the two initials, S. K. "My word. Who did that to that poor manatee?"

"Every time I see it I want to cry and hit the scum with a ball bat who carved his initials there," the Manatee Girl said. "Isn't that awful?"

"Awful," Mandy said as she looked at the manatee. When Mandy turned to Jill, she saw the young girl's blue eyes were shiny with tears.

Jill spoke. "That just hurts me that someone could be so cruel. These creatures are like gentle giants. They don't hurt anyone. They have no enemies except for boats. To think that poor Tubs had to endure some stupid kid carving his initials into his back. The manatee could have flipped around and knocked that kid to the bottom of the ocean. I wish he had. Poor Tubs is too gentle for his own good."

Mandy nodded. "That's the most awful thing I ever saw. Couldn't they arrest the person who did that?"

A voice from behind them answered the question. It was Crosslin. "Yes, they can now," he answered.

Mandy jumped. "I tried to wake you, but you were really sawing logs."

Crosslin looked puzzled.

Mandy giggled. "In Oklahoma, sawing logs means making noise while you're sleeping ."

Jill smiled at Crosslin. "Hi, Log Sawer."

"Hi," Crosslin said and blushed. "Well, Mandy, this is Jill. Jill, this is Mandy Miller." Mandy could tell that Crosslin had a crush on Jill by the way he looked at her.

"I was just telling Mandy about Tubs and what happened to him," explained Jill. "They did this a long time ago. I'll always remember those stupid initials, 'S. K.'"

"That boy must truly hate manatees to cut into one like that," Mandy said.

Crosslin nodded. "He's probably the one who hung out the sign."

"What sign?" Mandy asked.

Crosslin shook his head. "You'll have to see it to believe it. Jill, can you go with us? I can have my sister drive us to the marina."

Jill looked at her watch. "I can go. I have two more hours before my mother comes home. She said she might be late today."

Jill moved to rub Tubs' head. "Poor Tubs. He could have died from infection."

"Why didn't he?" Mandy asked.

"My grandfather saved him," Crosslin answered. "He dove down into the water and put herbs he uses as medicine on the cut. He doctored Tubs' back until it was well. That's why the manatee lived."

"When did he do that?" Mandy asked.

"When he was younger. He still has the pouch of salve he had mixed up. He has told that story many times. That's how I know. He's a great man."

Mandy hoped she could get to know Crosslin's grandfather. He was Indian. Her grandfather was Indian, too, but he had died right after her dad had died. To have a grandfather who could tell you stories would be pretty neat.

Jill's teeth clenched. "Do you think your grandfather has seen that awful sign? I heard about it. I want to see it!"

Crosslin looked concerned. "The more I think about it, the more I think it will be too upsetting for you."

"I want to see the sign," Jill repeated.

"I want to see it, too, Crosslin. Jill can handle seeing it." Mandy grinned at Jill. "Can't you?" Mandy didn't know what the sign said, but with Crosslin talking about the sign this way she sure didn't want to miss seeing it.

"Yeah. I can handle it," Jill said.

"How would we get there?" Mandy asked.

Crosslin chuckled. "My sister. I'll mow the grass for her. That will be a good bribe."

The three hurried to Crosslin's house so he could make arrangements for the ride to the marina.

"We'll wait out here while you talk to your sister," Jill said.

Crosslin grinned. "Wish me luck. Fawn is tough."

Mandy watched Crosslin go into the house. When he returned, his sister was with him. She was twirling the car keys ring around her index finger.

Crosslin introduced Fawn to Mandy and Jill.

Fawn turned to Crosslin, "So little brother, you'll mow the lawn for me. Both front and back?"

"Yeah, the entire lawn," Crosslin said.

They climbed into the car and fifteen minutes later, they were in front of the marina. As they climbed out of the car, Mandy wondered what the sign could say that would cause both Jill and Crosslin to become upset. Then Mandy saw the sign. Jill, the Manatee Girl, saw it, too, because tears were rolling down her pale cheeks. The banner was tied from post to post. The letters were at least six inches tall and were black on a red background. The sign read: "Eat a Manatee for Lunch."

Chapter Two

Mandy watched the Manatee Girl's face. It was lipstick red with rage. "Come on you two," Jill said. "Help me take this dumb sign down."

They quickly untied the banner. Crosslin rolled it up.

Mandy spotted an empty barrel that was turned over. "Give it here," she said. She quickly slid the banner under the empty barrel.

Hearing the sound of a door closing on a nearby yacht, Crosslin whispered, "Someone's coming. Let's get out of here."

"I'm not leaving until I talk to the dirty dog that hung up that sign," Jill said.

Mandy grabbed Jill's arm. "We know how you feel, but this is not the time to fight. We better leave before we get in trouble."

Jill kept pulling away, but Mandy hung tightly onto Jill's arm. Mandy wasn't giving up until she had the Manatee Girl next to the car.

"Get into the car, everybody," Crosslin ordered.

They all jumped into the car.

Mandy looked out the back window of the car. She saw a tall boy coming from a big yacht. They could have gotten caught. She felt her heart pounding and wondered if Crosslin's, Jill's and Fawn's hearts were pounding, too.

Crosslin's sister pulled away burning rubber.

"Gosh, Fawn," Crosslin said, "that was a nice quiet getaway."

"Sorry," his sister said.

They all giggled nervously.

"We've got to do something or all the boaters who stay at that marina won't care about the manatees and just butcher them with their boat's propeller. They won't even slow down or watch for them. They'll think it's funny instead of serious," Jill said.

"Where to now, Crosslin?" Fawn asked.

"Home. We need to talk to Grandfather," Crosslin said. "He'll give us good advice."

Jill glanced at her watch. "I still have plenty of time."

"Does your mother work?" Mandy asked.

"She used to," Jill said, "but she doesn't now."

"Where is she? Is she home? Do you need to call her?" Mandy asked.

Jill shook her head. "No, she isn't home," Jill said. "She's with my little sister."

"How old is your sister?" Mandy asked.

"Six," Jill said.

"What's her name?" Mandy asked.

"My little sister's name is Clarice. We call her Clarie."

"Does she have long, blonde hair like yours?" Mandy asked.

Jill's eyes became cloudy.

Is she crying? Why would she be crying? Mandy wondered,

Jill looked at the ground shaking her head. "No," she said. "Not like mine."

They followed Crosslin into his house.

Jill turned around. "Where is your grandfather?" she asked as if she wanted to change the subject. "We really need to talk to him."

Mandy wondered why Jill was upset. Who knew? Maybe her sister was visiting out of town during spring break and Jill was missing her.

"I'll get Grandfather," Crosslin said.

Mandy looked at the Manatee Girl. "I know your first name is Jill. What is your last name?"

"Winters. Jill Winters."

"I'll give you my Nana's telephone number, and you give me your number," Mandy said.

Jill blushed and mumbled. "We don't have a telephone. I'll have to call you."

Mandy knew Jill didn't want to talk about something, and Mandy knew that something was they didn't have money for a phone or some kind of a problem. Her grandmother said it helped to talk out your problems. Maybe if they became close, Jill would talk to her about whatever was bothering her.

Crosslin's grandfather walked into the room. Mandy couldn't believe he was so tall and lean. His long gray hair was braided on each side instead of pulled back like Crosslin's. His face had many wrinkles, and Mandy knew he was probably at least 80.

"My grandson said you have a problem with the boaters. Tell me your problem."

"Grandfather, have you seen the sign at the marina?" Crosslin asked.

"About the manatees?" the old man asked.

"Yes, Grandfather," Crosslin said.

"Sorry sign," the old man said.

"Yes, Grandfather, it is a sorry sign," Crosslin said.

"Is that where you went?" he asked

"Yes, Grandfather, we went to the marina. We took the sign down and hid it."

"Did anyone see you?" he asked.

"No one saw us," Crosslin said.

Mandy wondered if the tall boy who was walking from the big boat had seen them. She didn't know so she said nothing.

"Not true. Someone always sees you," Grandfather said.

Mandy turned to Crosslin's grandfather. "Did anyone see the boy who carved the initials on the manatee's back?" she asked.

Grandfather nodded. "I was swimming. I slipped out when they came and saw him use the knife to carve initials into the manatee's back. It was an awful sight. I grabbed a rock and hurled it at the boy with the knife. The rock hit the boy's forehead right about here," he said touching just below the hairline. "That boy is now a man and he will carry a scar just as the manatee does."

"How do you know it made a scar?" the Manatee Girl asked.

Crosslin chuckled. "In the woods, my grandfather could knock a squirrel out of a tree with a rock. It would be dead. Grandfather told us the boy's forehead bled badly. It made a scar."

Grandfather shook his finger at the Manatee Girl. "You look for the man with a scar. He will be easy to find because he will wear his shame like a blanket."

"What about the other boy?" Crosslin asked. "Didn't you say he was older?"

Grandfather nodded. "The other boy was older. He told the younger one what to do. I will never forget their faces nor will they forget mine. Now we must help the manatees."

"How Grandfather?" Crosslin asked.

"You must learn the wolf's way then you will know how to fight him."

"The wolf's way?" Mandy asked.

"Yes. The wolf spots a victim, then enlists his friends to help, and they circle the victim and charge from all directions. First one direction, a nip or bite and then another will do injury until they have the victim worn down. That is how you will fight the wolf. With his own tactics."

"But Grandfather, we can't do that. We can't attack the wolf. These people are rich!"

"That's true, but money can't pay for the lives of manatees. You three must be like little foxes. You must be crafty. You must find something those wealthy boat owners love more than their boats. You find this and you will have your answer."

"Sure," Crosslin said.

Mandy could see the disappointment on her two new friends' faces. Jill looked as discouraged as Crosslin.

"Come on you two, come next door to Nana's. She'll fix us some sandwiches. She baked a chocolate cake for me. Maybe we can think better on a full stomach."

As they walked next door and went inside, Mandy called, "Nana, I have someone for you to meet. Crosslin and Jill are with me."

Mandy looked through the house. She saw a note. "Our neighbor, Mrs. Mills was stranded at the doctor's office so she called for me to come get her. Sandwich stuff in refrigerator. Cake under cake keeper. Feed Crosslin too. Love Nana."

"I'll fix our lunch." Mandy opened the refrigerator to gather the ingredients to make sandwiches. "I do this at home all the time. My mama works, and I have to fix dinner a lot."

"Do you have enough for me, too?" Jill asked, shyly. "I don't have to eat."

"Of course. Nana has tons of food." Mandy quickly fixed three fat sandwiches of shaved turkey and cut three wide slices of chocolate cake. She poured orange juice into three glasses. "I love the orange juice in Florida. It's simply heavenly. Okay, let's figure out what your grandfather said so we'll find our answer. He said the wolf would give us the answer. Let's figure it out. What do we know?"

"They howl at night," Jill said.

"They run in packs." Crosslin chimed in.

"But what he was really saying was that we have to find what the boat owners love more than their boats," Mandy said. "That is what we must use."

"Love more than their boats. What would that be?" Jill asked.

The three suddenly became quiet trying to figure out the puzzle. Mandy looked around the room searching for an answer. The extra package of stars was on the kitchen cabinet. "I know. I know. I know the answer."

"What?"

"The thing they love more than their boat is their children and their grandchildren."

"Yes," Crosslin said making fists out of his hands.

"You're right," Jill said.

"Now, how are we going to get to know the children and grandchildren?" Mandy asked.

"Most of them are staying on the boats with their grandparents. They hang around the marina," Crosslin said.

"I wish we had a yacht we could pull into the marina, and we could invite the kids over to play games and get to know us," Jill said taking a sip of orange juice. "Then we could take them down to meet the manatees."

"We don't have anything but a canoe," Crosslin said. Crosslin's eyes lit up. "I know who will help. Grandfather has a friend, Big Bear. He has a yacht. He's Seminole Indian. He's very rich from oil wells in Oklahoma. He winters here. Big Bear has a telephone on his boat. Grandfather has the number. We can call him."

"Do you think he'll help us?" Mandy asked.

Crosslin nodded. "You bet. Big Bear loves animals, especially the manatees."

"Let's go next door and call him," Jill said.

"Let me leave Nana a note so she'll know where I am," Mandy said.

Mandy scribbled a quick note, and the three of them raced next door to call Big Bear.

Crosslin pointed. "Here it is on the wall. Grandfather has all his friends' telephone numbers on the wall." Crosslin quickly dialed. "His phone isn't working. Let's ask grandfather how we can get a message to Big Bear."

"Is your grandfather still here?" Mandy asked.

"He's out back. He likes to stay outdoors." Crosslin pushed the screen door open to the back yard, and the two girls followed.

Mandy saw his grandfather sitting on a wooden chair in the back yard. His hands were on top of the cane in front of him.

They hurried to the elderly man's side.

"Grandfather," Crosslin said, "come help us. We need to reach Big Bear. His phone doesn't work. Can you send smoke signals to him?"

The old man tapped his cane on the ground. "Not from here in town. The fire engine would be here in five minutes. We can go to the hill on the edge of town, and I'll signal him. We used to do this back home when we were kids. The other kids weren't interested in old Indian ways, but we were different. Let me get some matches and paper. You kids can gather the wood. Crosslin, bring my old blanket from the back porch."

"Can any of you drive?" Grandfather asked, joking.

The three shook their heads.

"I can try," Crosslin said.

Grandfather chuckled. "My heart couldn't take it. Your sister can drive." A wide grin creased his face.

Fawn appeared twirling the car keys around her index finger. "Are you talking about me? Do you want to go somewhere, Grandfather?"

"Yes," he said as Crosslin helped him stand. "I will ride in the front seat with you, Fawn. The scout is always in the front."

Mandy grinned. She sure liked Crosslin's grandfather.

They walked slowly to the car with Crosslin holding on to his grandfather's arm. Fawn burned rubber taking off again.

Mandy looked at Jill and shook her head. They both giggled. In thirty minutes, they were on the hill.

Everyone scrambled out of the car and began to gather twigs, wood, and dried leaves. Grandfather soon had a good fire going.

"I should have brought marshmallows and wire hangers to roast them on," Mandy said.

"Next time," Grandfather said.

Grandfather began waving the blanket over the fire, sending puffs of smoke into the air.

"What did your smoke signal say?" Crosslin asked.

"Call Rabbit Who Hops."

"He'll see it. He's on his big boat and the sky is clear. He'll see it,"

Crosslin said.

"Let's get home, Grandfather, so you can get Big Bear's call," Fawn said.

The telephone was ringing as they walked into the house. "Put it on the speakerphone, Crosslin. I know it is Big Bear."

"Hello," Grandfather said.

"This Big Bear. Are you Rabbit Who Mops?"

"No, this is Rabbit Who Hops, you stupid old man."

"Me, stupid? You never could get the 'H' to stay together. It always ends up like a M."

Both men laughed deep laughs.

"What can I do for my oldest friend?" Big Bear asked over the speakerphone.

"Do you have your boat here in Vero Beach," Crosslin's grandfather asked.

"Yes. Why?"

"My grandson and his friends are cooking up a plan and need your help. I'll put Crosslin on."

Soon the Manatee Team had their plans made with Big Bear.

Jill and Crosslin looked so hopeful that Mandy began to worry. Would their plans work? Maybe. Maybe not. A lot was at stake.

Chatper Three

Within the hour, Big Bear had his yacht moored at the very marina where the banner had waved. Mandy, Crosslin and Jill were on the marina waiting to climb aboard.

Big Bear was as tall as Crosslin's grandfather. He looked more like a business executive with his hair cut short. "Welcome," he yelled as he pushed a button and the gangplank went down so they could walk onto the yacht. "My home is your home."

"Wow," Mandy whispered to Crosslin. "What a break to get to spend time on this big boat."

Mandy couldn't believe a boat could be so beautiful. It was white, trimmed in navy blue. Crosslin had informed her that boats this large were called yachts. It had a galley, which Big Bear explained was a kitchen, and staterooms that were bedrooms. They were standing in the rear, which Big Bear explained was the aft of the yacht. It could sleep ten easily.

Mandy was amazed that people could live in such luxury. It was like a dream being invited to play on this big boat.

"What games do we need?" Mandy asked. In her grandmother's closet she had seen Monopoly and Old Maid Cards.

"Games? Did you say games? I have all the latest video games," Big Bear said as he opened a cabinet full of video games. He opened another cabinet that held the board games: Operation, Rummikub, and Clue. Stacked on top of the board games were Old Maid Cards. Big Bear waved the Old Maid Cards. "I hate these cards. I end up with that old woman every time. If you want other games I will have them delivered to us here on the boat."

"Boat? It's more like a ship," Crosslin said.

Jill just looked and shook her head.

"Young lady, what do you think of Big Bear's toy?"

Jill said, "I never dreamed I would be on a boat like this. Could I bring my little sister later? She would love this."

"Bring her now. Go home and get her, and we'll all eat together on the deck."

Jill looked confused. "I . . . I can't. Maybe some other time."

"Why not?" Mandy asked, still excited about being on the boat. She wished her little sister, Summer, could be here with her.

Jill stammered, "She's not home." Her eyes pleaded for them not to ask more questions.

"Where is . . . " Crosslin started to ask when Mandy bumped his side.

Mandy headed to the other end of the boat. "Come on, Crosslin. Look at this."

When he got to her, Mandy whispered to Crosslin, "Can't you tell Jill doesn't want to tell us where her little sister is."

"You mean she won't tell us," Crosslin said.

Mandy pleaded, "Don't pry. She'll tell us when she's ready."

They hurried back to Jill and Big Bear.

"What are our plans?" Mandy asked.

Big Bear stood very straight. He held his head high. His voice boomed, "Well, I want to say to you three, I think you're amazing kids to want to help the manatees. The manatees are like my brother. I feel badly that they are being killed. Soon, they are going to be like the red man. Gone."

Mandy liked Big Bear's looks. He was probably 6' 4" tall. His dark hair had very little gray in it. Mandy knew he was probably the same age as Crosslin's grandfather, but he looked much younger. Mandy wondered if people with easy lives aged less.

"I have seen many people disrespect Mother Earth, Brother Sky and Sister Stream." The man looked like he might cry. "They fill the skies with pollutants. They dump chemicals into the mouth of Mother Earth and they seep into our water supplies. They dump waste from their factories and toilets into our water. They then wonder why their children get sick.

"Their carelessness angers Mother Earth. Sometimes her anger comes forth as an earthquake, flood or volcano. Mother Earth is getting fed up," Big Bear said.

Jill walked over to Big Bear and took his hand. "Careless people are killing my friends, the manatees."

"I know. We must fight them. We must circle our wagons," Big Bear said.

Mandy looked at Crosslin and Big Bear and began to giggle.

Then Jill and Crosslin began to laugh as well.

"What's so funny, you three?" Big Bear asked.

Crosslin said, "Big Bear, it's the white men who circled their wagons, not the Indians."

Big Bear laughed a deep laugh. "Well, if it worked for them, it will work for us."

Mandy giggled. Big Bear was funny. She liked Crosslin, and she especially liked Jill.

Some children had walked over to the yacht and were admiring it.

Mandy poked Jill. "Those kids could be future members of our manatee group."

"Yeah," Jill said. "What are our plans?"

Mandy, Jill, Crosslin and Big Bear all put their heads together and whispered until their plans were made. Starting Monday they would meet at the marina at 10 a.m. They would befriend the kids from the marina, and then they would take them to meet the manatees. Jill would introduce each manatee to the children so the marina kids would know each manatee personally. Hopefully, the children would hound their parents and grandparents to drive their boats slowly to avoid hitting the manatees.

"Why aren't we meeting tomorrow?" Mandy asked.

"It's the Lord's day," Big Bear said. "Crosslin's family will be in church. Your grandmother goes to the same church, so I'll probably see you there, too. We'll start on our project Monday early."

Big Bear was right. Sunday morning, her grandmother woke her up early for church. When she got there, she saw Big Bear and his wife, June, and Crosslin and his family. As they were walking out, she looked around hoping to see Jill. She wasn't there. She wondered if she went to church anywhere.

Back in Oklahoma, Mama always slept late since it was her only day off. Then she cleaned house and did laundry. When Daddy was alive, they always went to church, but things were different now. Mama seemed to be in a fog. It was like she was heartsick and had given up. Not only did they never go to church, they never did anything anymore.

The plan was that Monday morning, Fawn would drive Crosslin and Mandy to the marina, and Jill would meet them there. She was so excited she could hardly sleep Sunday night. Finally Monday did come and Jill was at the marina waiting.

Big Bear's voice boomed. "We have donuts, if anyone is hungry." Although they all had eaten breakfast, they hurried to the table and had big glazed donuts with Big Bear and June.

Mandy motioned for Jill and Crosslin. "Let's go down and get to know the marina kids. Then we'll invite them to play a game."

Soon, Mandy, Crosslin and Jill had joined the kids chasing the tiny lizards that darted quickly along the marina and shoreline. Mandy had great fun chasing the little lizards. A few lizards were in a wire cage the size of a small lunch pail.

After Crosslin had caught three lizards and put them in the cage he asked, "What do you do with these at the end of the day?"

"I don't know," one of the kids answered.

"Why don't we make a plan to release the lizards at night, so they don't die in the cage," Crosslin suggested. "We can catch them again tomorrow."

"Yeah," the children said.

"That's a good plan," one boy said.

"Someone should be in charge of releasing them," Crosslin said.

"I say we should poke their eyes out and let them run around blind," a tall kid wearing the latest mall clothes and expensive looking tennis shoes said.

Mandy looked at the boy in shock. He had a cruel look about him with his piercing black eyes and black hair. What was wrong with this kid's thinking? How could anyone hurt helpless little creatures? "What's your name?" Mandy asked.

"Thurston. Why do you ask?"

Mandy shrugged. "I don't know," she said but knew she certainly didn't want to know him too well.

The boy puffed out his chest and sneered, "Thurston Winston III. What's your name?"

"Why do you ask?" Mandy asked.

"Beats me because I don't really care," Thurston said and turned and walked off. He climbed aboard a big yacht.

"Big Bear's yacht is bigger," Crosslin commented. Mandy and Jill agreed.

"Yeah. You guys' yacht is bigger," the kids agreed.

Mandy straightened up tall. She started to say something like it's not our yacht, but she liked the idea that it was. Being on the yacht was like having a sweet dream and not wanting the dream to end.

A boy who needed a haircut walked up to Mandy. He looked to be about twelve. His wet hair was parted and combed neatly. His clothes were well worn but clean.

"Hello, I'm Mandy. What's your name?"

"Butch Simpson."

"Is Butch your real name?" Mandy asked.

Butch shrugged. "No, but that's what my family calls me. I like it better than Orville, which is my real name. I'll let the lizards out at night. That's a good idea because they're usually dead in the cage the next morning."

"I wonder why they die?" Mandy asked.

Big Bear appeared at Mandy's side. "If they put you in the broiling sun without water or food, you would die, too."

Mandy shuddered. "I would hate to be in a cage."

Butch looked at them. "Me, too. Some of the lizards dropped their tails off to get away, but the kids knew their tricks and caught them anyway. They've caught about six. I promise I'll free them."

Mandy liked this boy. He had a good heart. She glanced at the middle of the marina. There was a long picnic table and children on benches around it playing board games. Soon Mandy, Jill and Crosslin knew all the names of the kids. They also knew who stayed on which boat. All but one were staying on their grandfather's boat. They were becoming good friends.

"Should we take them to see the manatees now?" Mandy whispered to Jill.

"No later. The kids need to know us better," Jill said.

"Hello," Ruby, the marina owner's daughter, called to them. She walked over to talk. She told them she was named Ruby because she had ruby red hair when she was born. Mandy got the impression that Ruby wasn't afraid of anybody or anything. She was thirteen. Mandy didn't get too friendly with Ruby because whenever they played Clue and Ruby lost, she would stomp off mad.

Megan was Ruby's younger sister. She was nine. She was quiet and sweet and seemed to be the apple of her father's eye.

Soon the children were called to their particular boat to eat and Big Bear called Mandy, Crosslin and Jill to lunch. "Well, little foxes how are we doing?" Big Bear asked.

Crosslin shrugged. "I can't tell."

"I can," Mandy said. "We need to make a list of who we think will love the manatees, and we'll ask permission to take them on a field trip to the McKee's Botanical Garden which they're restoring. Once we are away from the marina, we can stop on the way, and let Jill call the manatees. Maybe they can get to know each manatee. That should help."

Jill looked worried. "Tomorrow could be a problem. If I'm able to come, I'll meet you in the canal behind the power plant."

Mandy began to worry. What if they got all the kids together and spent time going through the garden, and Jill couldn't meet them to call the manatees. What would they do?

After they ate, Crosslin's sister came after them. Mandy was soon home. She told her grandmother about the plan they had to help the children become acquainted with the manatees. "Nana, what if Jill doesn't get to come to call the manatees?"

"Have I met Jill?"

"No. Nana, people call her the Manatee Girl because she can call the manatees to her."

Nana smiled. "Perhaps you could have Crosslin's grandfather go with you. He might be the answer to that problem. He's a wise old man. He has lots of stories he can tell."

Mandy had told Nana what Big Bear said about circling the wagons and her grandmother thought it was funny, too.

"Nana, do you want to go?"

"I think it would be better if you weren't covered up with adults so you have room to circle your wagons. Besides, I'm working on a surprise for you. It will give me a chance to finish it."

Mandy put her face so close to her grandmother's their noses were touching. "What is it, Nana? Tell me," Mandy pleaded.

Grandmother stepped back and shook her head. "If I tell, it won't be a surprise. I will tell you this, Crosslin's grandmother taught me to make them. She died last year, but I still hear Crosslin talking with her."

"Talking with her? I thought she was dead."

"Some Indian people visit with their ancestors. Sometimes, Crosslin sits on the back step and talks to his grandmother when he is troubled. I've heard him."

"Does she hear him?" Mandy asked.

"I'm sure she does. You'll have to ask him," her grandmother said.

"Mandy, I'm a little concerned about Fawn driving you kids around. If you're going more than a few blocks I would rather a grown-up drive. I'd be glad to drive, but my car is rather small."

Mandy smiled. "Nana, Big Bear is taking his big passenger van. We'll be fine."

Her grandmother returned her smile. "That's good. I'll quit worrying. Mandy, ask Big Bear to tell you children how he was named. It's a good story."

"Tell me, Nana," Mandy said.

Mandy's grandmother shook her head. "No. It's Big Bear's story. He'll have to tell it." She laughed a deep laugh. "You'll like it."

Mandy was curious about Big Bear's name. The way her grandmother laughed, it must be funny.

Mandy's grandmother helped her call her mother. Mandy visited with both her mother and Summer. She told them all about Jill, Crosslin and the manatees.

Mother seemed relieved to finally talk to Mandy. Her mother told her she had tried to call several times and never found them home. Summer said, "Sissy, come home right now."

Mandy laughed. She knew she could get Summer's mind off track real easy, and her little sister would quit begging her to come home. "What are you doing in nursery class?"

Summer quickly told her of the plaster plate they were making of their handprint.

"Is that for Mother for Mother's Day?" Mandy asked.

It worked for a little while, but Summer must really miss her to keep asking her to come home.

"In a few days. Summer, I'll bring you a present. Will that make you happy?"

"Yeah, but come home now," Summer insisted.

"I'll be back in a few days with a present. Will you come to the airport with Mother?"

"Yeah. I'll be there. Sissy, I miss you."

"Summer, I miss you, too." Soon, Mother took the phone back and they said their good-byes. Mandy and her grandmother had a light dinner. Mandy put on her pajamas and crawled into bed.

Try as she may, she couldn't settle down. All she could think about were the manatees being cut open by the propeller of the speeding boats. Some had gaping wounds in their backs that looked like raw hamburger meat. At last, she fell asleep, but dreamed a troubling dream. She dreamed that the manatee spoke and said, "I don't hurt anyone. Help me. Help me."

Mandy woke up breathless. Her heart pounded. When she realized where she was, she crawled out of bed and hurried down the hall. She knocked, then pushed the door open slightly as her grandmother switched on a lamp.

"Honey, are you homesick?" her grandmother asked.

"No, Nana. I just had a bad dream."

"Do you want to talk about it?"

Mandy shook her head. "No. If I tell it before breakfast it might come true."

"Who told you that?"

"My other grandmother."

"Oh," her grandmother said and smiled. "Well then you better wait until after breakfast."

"Nana, may I crawl in bed with you?"

"Sure, Sugar. Maybe you won't have any more bad dreams."

Mandy sure hoped so. The nightmare dreams were wearing her out. Sleeping in grandmother's bed didn't help. As soon as Mandy went to sleep she dreamed the children got angry because the Manatee Girl wasn't there to call the manatees to shore. They said they hated the manatees for causing the boats to have to slow down. In her dream, Thurston passed out sticks to poke out the manatees' eyes. She screamed, "Don't do that. They don't hurt anyone. Don't hurt them!"

"Mandy, wake up," her grandmother said. "My, but you have a lot of worries walking around in your mind. Don't worry, I'll have your present finished tomorrow. After that, you'll have no more bad dreams."

"Okay, Nana." Mandy settled in and soon drifted into a light sleep.

The next morning Mandy was up eating breakfast when Crosslin tapped on the screen door. "Are you ready?" he called through the screen.

"Almost. Come in. Do you want some cereal?"

"I've eaten," Crosslin said.

Mandy chased the last three Cheerios around the bowl of milk with her spoon. "There, I got them."

Crosslin looked puzzled. "Got who?"

"The last three Cheerios. I always have three little round donuts that try to get away."

Crosslin nodded. "I know what you mean. My mom gets on to me, but I drink the bowl of milk. I get them that way."

"I do that, too. My mom gets on to me because she says it's bad manners. It's sort of a game with me. Me against the Cheerios. I wonder if Jill drinks her cereal milk like we do?"

"Don't know," Crosslin said.

"Do you think Jill will be at the canal? If she is, I'll ask her."

Locking his arms in front, Crosslin said, "I don't know. I think it depends on her family. She'll be there if she can."

Mandy stretched, "I'm still tired. I didn't get much sleep."

"How come?" Crosslin asked.

"I had a bad dream," Mandy explained.

"What was your dream about?" Crosslin asked. "Sometimes my grandfather dreams warnings."

"I'm not going to say. I just hope that Thurston kid isn't coming with us. He was in my dream." Mandy called to her grandmother, "Nana, we're getting ready to leave."

"I'm coming," Nana said coming into the room and kissed her. "I was packing you kids a picnic lunch."

"That's great, Nana. Thanks. We probably won't be back until evening. Will that be okay?"

"Sure. There's enough food for your friends, too." She handed Mandy a large straw picnic basket with handles.

Mandy wondered if the marina kids would come. Did they like her and Crosslin and Jill enough to be considered friends? She hoped so.

Meeting the manatees a few times would give the children from the marina a chance to get to know the gentle giants by name. When they met each one of the manatees, surely they would want to help save them.

Smiling, Mandy lifted the basket. "Wow, Nana. This is heavy. What's in here?"

Her grandmother smiled, "Cold drinks, fried chicken, buttered bread and sliced apples. You can keep it in the car until after your tour of the botanical garden. The workers and volunteers have worked hard to bring the garden back to life. When your grandfather and I moved here years ago, the garden had orchids and parrots. It was a show place."

"It has been overgrown with vines and brush since I've lived here," Crosslin said.

"Crosslin, you wouldn't have known it. It had birds of every description and beautiful flowers, then it was neglected for years and became like a jungle."

"Nana, have they fixed it?"

"Yes, they have. It's quite beautiful already, but they're still working on it."

"When a hurricane comes through it blows down large trees, and they have to be removed by heavy equipment. They have to replace and replant whatever is damaged. They don't have the birds and orchids of the past, but the garden is still very special. You'll enjoy the tour."

"Nana, are you sure you don't mind me leaving?"

Her grandmother smiled, "Not at all. I need to do some shopping, pay some bills and work on your surprise. I'll do that while you're gone."

"Love you, Nana," Mandy said.

"Love you, too," her grandmother replied.

Crosslin walked toward Mandy. He reached for the basket. "I'll take the food basket." He chuckled. "I like to stay near the food. My sister will take us to the marina, and Big Bear will drive us on the field trip."

Mandy looked at her grandmother. "Is that okay, Nana?"

"It isn't far. Just ask Fawn to drive carefully," her grandmother said.

"Your telephone is ringing," Crosslin said.

"I bet that's my mother calling," Mandy replied.

"Mandy, it's for you." Grandmother pushed the receiver toward her. "It's your friend, Jill."

Mandy took the receiver from her. "Hi Jill. Did you get a phone?"

"No, I'm with my mother and sister, and I found a telephone I could use. Mandy, I hate to tell you this, but something came up and I won't be able to meet with you guys today. I'm so sorry. I just can't."

"Oh, Jill. That's terrible. That will mess up our plan. Nana fixed a picnic lunch for all the kids from the marina who are going on the field trip and then you were supposed to call the manatee to shore for them. Are you sure you can't get away? I can ask Nana to pick you up to meet us behind the power plant. We're going to the gardens first."

"No, I can't," Jill said.

"Why not? Can you tell me why?" Mandy begged.

"I don't have much time to talk. I'm real sorry," Jill said.

Mandy heard someone say to Jill, "We need you now." Then Mandy heard a click. The phone was dead.

Mandy stuck her fists in her sides. "She's not coming and wouldn't say why. Here we knock ourselves out to help her save her manatees, and then she lets us down. I can't believe it."

Crosslin shook his head. "Why do you think they're her manatees?"

"Because she loves them and they seem to love her."

"You sound jealous," Crosslin said.

"Maybe I am," Mandy admitted.

"Mandy, the manatees belong to no one," Crosslin said. "They are a free gift for us to love and enjoy but also to guard and protect. If we don't help them the manatees will be gone. We shouldn't be mad at Jill. She would be here if she could. I think something heavy is going down with her family."

"I think so, too. You're probably right, but why won't she tell us? I heard someone say to Jill, that they needed her now, so I guess it isn't her fault that she can't be with us. Maybe she'll tell us later."

Crosslin smiled, "Don't count on it. I've known her for two months, and she almost never talks about her family."

Mandy nodded. "You're right. Something is going on. Since she isn't going to tell us, maybe we'll have to plan something different today. After we tour the botanical garden, we'll have Big Bear and your grandfather tell us stories. We need to ask Big Bear how he got his name."

Crosslin grinned. "Yeah. That would be fun."

Fawn honked and Mandy and Crosslin hurried out to the car.

Fawn raised a large sack up in the air. "Grandfather had me fix a dozen peanut butter and jelly sandwiches, and he had me bring a sack of oranges. He's already at the marina. Big Bear picked him up earlier to have breakfast with him and his wife, June."

In a few minutes Fawn pulled into the parking lot. When Mandy and Crosslin got out of the car, Mandy saw all the marina kids gathered around Big Bear. He was doing magic tricks for them. Mandy knew most of the children, but there were others that she had never met.

"Hi," Ruby said. "I bet you wonder where all these kids came from. More boats docked this morning, and the people had their grandchildren with them. We told the kids we were going on a field trip, and they asked if they could come, too."

"Do you think Big Bear will mind?" Ruby asked.

"Naw," Crosslin said. "The more the merrier with Big Bear."

Mandy looked closely. She knew Ruby and her sister Megan.

"Hi," a voice behind her said. Mandy turned around to see Butch. Today he looked different. He had a fresh haircut and his clothes looked new.

"You look nice, Butch," Mandy said.

"Thanks. My grandparents came in on their big boat. The first thing they did was take me to get my hair cut. They bought me some new clothes, too. My mother died last year.

Since my dad works late every night, the barber shops are closed by the time he gets home."

"I'm glad you're coming Butch. You like manatees, don't you?"

"I sure do," Butch said.

Mandy's eyes searched the marina area. Thank goodness that cruel Thurston wasn't there. In her dream he had poked out the manatees' eyes. She didn't want him anywhere near the manatees. Two girls and three boys who Mandy had never seen were going. They all looked nice.

She breathed a sigh of relief that she didn't see Thurston. Maybe he wasn't coming along.

"Are you looking for me?" a voice behind her asked.

Mandy's heart sank. She recognized Thurston's voice and turned to face him. "Are you going on the field trip with us?" she asked hoping against hope that he wasn't coming.

"Yeah," Thurston replied. "I am and what are you going to do about it?"

Before Mandy could answer, Ruby said, "Thurston, I heard you say we were all dorks, and you weren't going."

"Well, I changed my mind," Thurston smirked.

"Well, maybe the rest of us dorks don't want to put up with you," Ruby said. Her green eyes were flashing.

"Too bad. Big Bear told me early this morning I could go, so I'm going."

Mandy felt helpless. Was her nightmare dream going to come true? There was nothing she could do to keep Thurston from coming with them.

Soon all the kids were in the van. The picnic basket and sack of sandwiches and oranges were in the back. Big Bear had brought a gallon of lemonade and lots of paper cups and a large bucket of fried chicken.

Soon they arrived. The tour guide explained the garden's history while walking through the trail of beautiful trees, bushes and flowers. Potatoes hanging by string-like vines from the treetops fascinated Mandy. The guide explained the vines were a problem in the garden because they grew so rapidly they could completely cover any nearby tree. The potatoes which fell to the ground were tossed into a basket to be disposed of later. It was important to prevent the fallen potatoes from growing. Over the years, it had taken a lot of effort to remove the potato vines.

Mandy was so glad she got to see the garden. When she had her own home, she wanted to have flowers just like the ones in this beautiful place.

After the tour of the botanical garden, they drove to Jaycee Park. Mandy ran ahead to spread a cloth on the picnic table. There were more children than places to sit, so Big Bear spread a blanket on the ground. "Some of you kids can eat on the blanket."

Thurston hurried to the table, but Ruby scooted ahead of him and all the seats were taken. He hurried to the chicken and took three of the best pieces. He then dropped to the blanket on the ground and ate his chicken. When he was finished, he tore his paper cup into little pieces and sprinkled them on the ground.

Big Bear looked down at the mess and said, "You are planning on picking that up, aren't you?" Thurston looked the other way, ignoring Big Bear.

Big Bear looked at Crosslin's grandfather and shook his head. He glared at Thurston. "Son, I don't think you heard me. I said either pick up that mess or walk home."

Thurston smirked. "Why?"

Big Bear pulled up to his full height and said, "You don't disrespect Mother Earth. Not in front of me. That's all I'll say and it better be cleaned up."

Thurston clenched his teeth and his face became apple red as he picked up the tiny pieces of drink cup from the ground.

Noticing that Thurston had missed several pieces, Mandy remembered what her grandmother had said about not littering, and she started picking up the pieces of cup.

"No, Mandy," Big Bear said. "Thurston will get them."

Thurston came back and snatched the remaining pieces of paper from the ground and dropped them into the trash container.

"Happy now?" he asked smartly.

"Yes," Big Bear said simply.

Soon every piece of chicken and every sandwich was eaten. Mandy had picked up the trash, folded the soiled tablecloth and put it back into the picnic basket.

"Are we ready to head to the canals?" Big Bear asked. "We don't have any food left."

The children all agreed it was time to leave and climbed into Big Bear's van. Crosslin's grandfather sat in the front with Big Bear and they laughed and talked about old times. When they got to the canals, they all sat on the grass along the bank.

Mandy looked at Crosslin's grandfather. He was sitting on the ground with all the children, but he sat cross-legged. She had never seen anyone this old sit like that.

"Big Bear, how did you get your name?" Mandy asked.

Big Bears eyes twinkled. "You really want to know?" he teased. When Mandy looked at Crosslin, his eyes were dancing with mischief. She knew this was going to be an interesting story.

"It is Indian custom for parents to name the child after the first thing they see. Well, my name is Big Bear. How come they named me Big Bear?"

"I bet I know," Ruby said. "You were born in the woods and your mother looked out the window and there was a big bear and they named you Big Bear."

"No, I was born in a hospital. Now, how was I named Big Bear?"

"Well, the hospital was in a wooded area and a wild bear came nearby and your mother saw it and named you Big Bear," Butch said.

Big Bear shook his head. "Does anyone else have any ideas? Crosslin, don't tell." Big Bear looked at Crosslin's grandfather. "Rabbit Who Hops, don't tell."

None of the other children had an idea.

"Tell us, Big Bear," Mandy pleaded.

"Okay, my parents decided I would be born in a hospital. My mother was in the delivery room a very long time and my father went down to the gift shop to look around. He bought my mother a large stuffed animal. It was not just large. It was huge. When my mother saw my father carrying that big stuffed white bear she said, 'Where in the world did you get that big bear?' Then she said, 'I know what our son's name will be. The first thing I saw was you carrying that big bear. From this day forth you will call my son, Big Bear.'"

The children laughed.

"Some Indian you are," Thurston said. "You're named after a stuffed toy. Why didn't they just call you, Big Fat Teddy Bear?"

"Perhaps they should have named you, Boy Without Manners," Big Bear answered.

"When you have as much money as my father has you don't have to have manners," Thurston sneered.

"Rich or poor, everyone needs to know to be courteous. Being rich is no excuse for being rude," Big Bear said.

"Thurston, why did you even come along? No one can stand you," Ruby said. "Call your daddy. Maybe he'll come and get you so we don't have to put up with you."

"They're cruising. They left early this morning. I'm staying with friends."

"I doubt that. You don't have any friends," Ruby said.

"Do too," Thurston said. "I'll show you. I'll call them." Thurston pulled out a cell phone from his pocket and dialed. "I need a ride home. Come get me at the canals behind the power plant. Right now." Pushing the button to hang up, he sneered. "See there. I do have a friend."

"They're not friends. Your daddy pays them to put up with you or they wouldn't come. You can bet on that," Ruby said.

Mandy knew what Ruby said was true, but she also knew those unkind words hurt Thurston's feelings. Mandy was beginning to feel sorry for him.

A few minutes later, a long black car honked. "They're here," Thurston said.

"See you around," Mandy called after him.

"Not if I see you dorks first," Thurston said as he climbed into the car.

"What a jerk," Crosslin said.

"I can't believe I felt sorry for him," Mandy said.

Rabbit Who Hops looked at the car as it pulled away. "Someone should feel sorry for the boy. He is carrying much sorrow inside."

Ruby sneered, "His rich mother dumped him when he was two. She never came back. His dad didn't want him so he pawned him off on his grandparents. They don't even like him."

"Pretty sorry state when grandparents don't love you," Rabbit Who Hops said.

Crosslin nodded. "Yes, grandfather. You're right."

Things were quiet. No one said a word. It was as if Thurston had ruined the happy mood of the day.

Mandy felt worried. She looked at Crosslin, and he seemed to pick up her thoughts. "Grandfather, can you tell us some stories?"

"What kind of stories?"

"About the manatees and the Indians," Crosslin said.

Grandfather nodded. "I'll tell you a story my grandfather told me. When Indians lived on the lands and there were no white people, the Indian people could speak the animals' languages. They would speak to the whales and the whales would sing. They sounded very much like women singing. The manatees didn't sing like the whales but made a different sound more like a squeak. One day the Indian people saw the smoke signals. They warned them of trouble coming.

"Another Indian tribe had been attacked by white men with big knives who got off a ship. The pirates killed many braves. The Indian people met with the animals of the sea and asked for their help. The whales said there are big rocks, and we will sing and lure them to the rocks. The manatees said when we sit up they will think we are women and we will lure their big boat into the rocks to wreck. They will no longer kill your people. Together the manatees and the whales lured the cutthroat pirates to the rocks and the ship was destroyed. Later the manatee and the whale said, 'No more. We will kill no more.'

"The Indians fought for a very long time and finally their chief said the same thing the manatee and whale said, 'No more. We will kill no more.'"

Crosslin's grandfather finished his story and things became quiet.

"Big Bear," Mandy said. "Is that why you said the manatee is like your brother?"

"Yes," Big Bear said. "The manatee is my brother. They saved my people. Now, we must save them," he said.

All the children sat in a circle and put their right hand on top of each other's. "Save the manatee," they chanted.

Mandy's heart felt so full she had to fight to keep the tears back. What a perfect day it had been, except for Thurston's rudeness.

As she looked toward the water, she wished Jill had been there to call the manatees to shore. Jill, where are you? She looked at the sky and saw storm clouds gathering. What if it rained for several days and they couldn't show the children the manatees. What if Jill never contacted them again? What if they never saw the Manatee Girl again?

Crosslin seemed to read Mandy's mind. "It's not going to rain and Jill will come back. We'll see her again."

"You're right," Mandy said but in her heart she wasn't sure he was right at all.

Chapter Four

After delivering the other children to their boats at the marina, Mandy was anxious to get home. She had so much to tell her grandmother. Big Bear's story about the manatees had gone straight to her heart. Mandy was sure all the children had been affected by the story. Perhaps now the group from the marina would feel closer to the manatees.

"Thanks for a great day, Big Bear," Mandy said as the van pulled in front of her grandmother's house.

"Thank your grandmother for the food she sent," Big Bear said.

"I will," Mandy said getting out of the car. She hurried into the house. "Nana, are you here?" she called.

A voice came from Mandy's bedroom, "In here. Come and look."

Mandy hurried down the hall into her bedroom. She saw her grandmother standing at the head of her bed.

"What do you think?" her grandmother asked as she pointed above the white wicker headboard to a wooden circle with thread woven across it.

Mandy wasn't sure what was hanging on the wall, but it reminded her of a spider web in a wooden frame. Colorful beads and feathers hung from rawhide strips hanging from each side.

"What is it, Nana?" Mandy asked. "It's beautiful."

"It's a Dream Catcher," her grandmother explained.

"What's a dream catcher?" Mandy asked.

Her grandmother smiled. "Indian people believe by hanging this over the headboard of your bed, you can filter out bad dreams and only the good dreams visit you while you sleep. You'll have no more bad dreams, Mandy. I promise."

Mandy touched the dream catcher. "Where did you get it?"

"I made it. Crosslin's grandmother, Willow, used to make them to sell at the local Powwows. Willow's dream catchers were the most beautiful. I wish she were still alive to help me make yours that special."

"Oh, Nana. I think it's the most beautiful thing I've ever seen."

Mandy's grandmother wrapped her arms around Mandy and pulled her close. "I want you to have only good dreams. This will help."

Mandy touched the feathers and beads that decorated the dream catcher. She felt so lucky to have a grandmother who loved her so much. She felt a little guilty for running off every day with Crosslin instead of visiting with her grandmother. "I'm sorry I've been gone so much, Nana."

"I don't mind one little bit. It would be boring for you hanging around this house all day. I'm delighted you've made some friends." She smiled, "Maybe next year you'll want to come back to visit me and them."

"I will, Nana. A lot happened today. I have so much to tell you." Mandy sat on the bed and told her grandmother about the trip to the garden and that every crumb of food was eaten.

"Did Big Bear tell his story?"

Mandy nodded. "He did and it was so funny but Thurston, that awful rich boy from the marina, was just a smarty pants about Big Bear's story."

"How was he smarty?" her grandmother asked.

"Well Big Bear told his story of why he was named Big Bear and we all loved it, but Thurston got right up in Big Bear's face and said, "They should have named you, Big Fat Teddy Bear.""

"Oh dear. That was out of line. Someone should teach that kid some manners," her grandmother said.

"Big Bear put Thurston in his place and he left in a huff," Mandy said. "I sort of felt sorry for him. No one loves him."

"Stay away from him," her grandmother warned. "If he doesn't get help, he will bring a lot of grief to those around him. He doesn't have to act that way. When I was young there was a young boy who came from the most awful family. They didn't love him, and they treated him terrible. He was the most loving, wonderful person. You don't have to act ugly because of your life. You choose to."

"That boy that was treated terrible. What happened to him?" Mandy asked.

"I married him and we were happy for 50 years. He always treated me so good because I treated him well. He died right after your father died. Your family couldn't come to the funeral because it was so far away and your mother had just started that new job. You remember him, don't you, Mandy?"

Mandy nodded. "Grandpa was so sweet to me. When I was eight, he took me every place with him and bought me ice cream. I remember he bought me a sack of malt balls and the bottom of the sack came loose and all the malt balls fell to the pavement and rolled away. I cried. He put me in the car and took me back to the mall to get more malt balls. Nana, you're right. He was a loving, wonderful person."

"Some boys are mean spirited and they don't want to be any different. Girls try to change them and end up unhappy. Stay away from that Thurston. He could be sweet if he wanted to be."

Mandy agreed. "Do you think he got his meanness from his father?" Mandy asked.

Grandmother shrugged. "Who knows? I've seen great parents have rotten kids. I've seen great kids come from rotten parents. You just never know."

"Nana, thanks for the dream catcher. I think I'll go to bed. I'm so tired."

"Sweet dreams," Grandmother said.

"Same to you, Nana," Mandy said.

The next morning, when Mandy awakened, she knew the dream catcher had helped because she had slept so well and had no bad dreams. She had heard the telephone ring one time and sat up in bed, but she heard her grandmother's voice talking to her friend. Mandy had hoped the call was from Jill or Crosslin. She wondered why she hadn't heard from them.

The day was boring. She watched some television, looked at the photo albums of her dad and felt lost without Crosslin and Jill. She walked next door to talk to Crosslin, but no one was at home, not even his grandfather. She kept repeating to herself all day, "Jill, call me. Jill, call me. I have so much to tell you."

She thought of her mother and little sister, Summer. Sometimes, Summer had bad dreams, too.

"Nana, could you show me how to make Summer a dream catcher? I promised her a present. I feel guilty that I'm here where it is so warm and beautiful. It's so cold back in Oklahoma."

"Sure, Honey. I've already started one for her. I'll show you how to make them. You might want to make them for your own children one day."

"I'd like that. Nana, tell me more about our Indian people."

Mandy's grandmother smiled. "My grandmother told me stories that her grandmother told her. She told me we must tell our grandchildren the stories so the truth doesn't die."

"What truth did she tell you, Nana?"

Mandy's grandmother's eyes became shiny with tears. "She told me that the Cherokee Tribe lived in Georgia. It was the most beautiful land of the United States. There were deer, wild game, and birds to hunt. The water was so clear, you could spear the fish with one try. The Cherokees never took more than they could use. They had everything they needed and wanted and life was good.

"Soon the settlers came and then miners found gold and then the problems began. I have something I want you to have, Mandy. You must give this to your child and tell them the story I am going to tell you.

"The soldiers were sent to take the Indians' land from them because it was so fertile and beautiful. Also gold was discovered in our homeland. Their plan was to move our people to a place called the Indian Territory. It would later be known as Oklahoma. Our people were brave and fought, but there came a time when our chief said as the manatees and whales said, 'We will kill no more.'

"Our people called the soldiers the 'Long Knives' because of their swords. So many soldiers came, and they soon overpowered our people.

"The Cherokees were marched a thousand miles. They walked across five states to get to what is now Oklahoma. Most of the old people and very young died. The Indian people would carry their dead and when they could carry no more they refused to walk so they could take care of their dead. Almost one-third of our people died. Probably more than 4,000."

Mandy shook her head in disbelief.

Her grandmother handed her a stone that was shaped like a perfect rose. Mandy looked at the red rose rock. She looked at her grandmother who stood so straight and realized how special she was. Her dark hair had little gray in it, and she wore it pulled to the back in a single braid. Her eyes were large and brown.

Remembering seemed to make her grandmother sad. Her eyes became shiny with tears. "Mandy, my grandmother told me the rose rock represents the Indian people who died on the trail of tears. It is red as our skin and strong as a rock and as beautiful as our people. My grandmother gave me this rock, and I now give it to you. You must tell the story to your children and pass the rock to them to pass to their children and our history will never die."

Mandy was only twelve but she knew this was a special moment. "Oh Nana, I love you so much. I'll take good care of this rose rock, and I'll give it to my child to pass on."

"You must tell them the story of the strength of our people to survive."

"I will, Nana. I promise. I'm glad we had this day to talk."

"Yes. It is a good day, but now the manatees need you. Tomorrow you and Crosslin and your friend, Jill, must continue with your plan. Your time here is running out and the manatees' time will soon run out if people don't help them."

"Nana, what if Jill never calls? We don't know how to reach her."

"Come outside with me," Grandmother said.

Mandy followed her grandmother out the back door to the back yard. Mandy's grandmother became very still, and she appeared to be listening. The wind had seemed to come up when they walked out the door.

"You will hear from your friend tomorrow," her grandmother said.

"Nana, how do you know?"

"Our people told me. When you are troubled, you can talk to our people. They will help you."

"What people?"

"Your Cherokee ancestors. They will help you."

They went inside the house and down the hall to Mandy's bedroom. Her grandmother kissed her goodnight and closed the bedroom door.

Mandy wasn't sure she believed this spooky stuff about talking to dead people, but she did believe in her grandmother. She felt so tired. When she climbed into bed, she was still thinking about Jill. She got up quickly and tiptoed to the window.

"If you're out there ancestors, I need you," she whispered. "We need Jill with us so we can save the manatees. If you're there, have her come tomorrow. We need her help." She crawled back into bed, not knowing if they had heard her, but she sure hoped they had.

The next morning Mandy was awakened by the sound of the cooing doves. Jumping up she ran to the window. Another day in paradise, she thought.

In the kitchen, she found her grandmother sitting at the table working on Summer's dream catcher.

"So, you're up," Grandmother said. "Did you sleep well?"

"Yes, I did!" Mandy exclaimed. "May I watch you make the dream catcher while I eat my cereal?"

"You bet," her grandmother said.

Mandy watched in amazement as Nana wove the string from side to side to form the spider-web like pattern. "Is that the part which stops the bad dreams?"

Her grandmother nodded. "It is the most important part. The feather and beads and rawhide strings are just decorations. This web keeps the bad dreams from entering your mind."

As Mandy watched her grandmother she began to think about her mother back in Tulsa. She was glad Mother had let her come to Vero Beach. She looked toward the phone. "I'm glad I talked to Mother. I know she misses me."

"Do you want to call her?"

Mandy looked at the clock. "No, Mom has already left for work. I don't want to bother her there. Has Crosslin been by?"

"Yeah. Twice. He thinks you're a real sleepyhead."

Mandy poured the cereal into her bowl and got the container of milk from the refrigerator. "What did he say?" she asked as she sat down and began to eat.

"Crosslin said Jill called, and will be at the canals at eleven. She plans on calling the manatees to shore. She wants Crosslin to ask Big Bear to drive the marina kids to the canals behind the power plant. She asked if you could come early so she could tell you something."

"What?" Mandy asked.

"I don't know. Ask Crosslin."

"Is she up yet?" Crosslin called through the screen door.

"Just a minute," Mandy said and ran down the hall and slipped into her shorts and T-shirt. She ran back to the table barefooted. "Come on in."

"I didn't think you were ever going to wake up," Crosslin said. "Did your grandmother tell you Jill called?"

"Yeah. That's great. What did she say?"

"Nothing other than she wants you at the canals before eleven."

"Why does she want me there first?" Mandy asked.

Crosslin smiled. "She needs to tell you where she has been. She told me, but she wants to tell you in person. Okay?"

"Okay," Mandy said.

"Fawn can drive us to the canals to see if Jill is there yet. Fawn took Grandfather earlier to have breakfast with Big Bear and June. Big Bear's going to load up his van with the kids from the marina to meet Jill and the manatees at the canals. Big Bear offered to take all of us cruising on his big boat afterwards. We have to get permission slips signed from the parents first, so I'll go to the marina and handle that."

Mandy gobbled down her breakfast and ran to get her tennis shoes. They would be less slippery on the boat. "Is Fawn ready?" she asked Crosslin.

"She's sitting on the porch with the car keys. She loves to drive us around and bribe me to do all her work."

Mandy giggled. "What do you have to do for her today?"

"The dinner dishes," he replied.

Mandy giggled. "Come get me after you've finished dinner, and I'll help you with the dishes."

Crosslin grinned. "That sounds like a deal," he replied.

Mandy kissed her grandmother and hurried out the door. Fawn had pulled into the driveway and Crosslin and Mandy got into the car. In a few minutes they were at the park. Mandy saw Jill. "She's there. Don't you want to say anything to her?" Mandy asked Crosslin.

Crosslin shook his head. "We talked by phone. She wants to talk to you alone. She already told me everything."

"Everything what? Tell me," Mandy pleaded as they pulled into the parking at the power plant.

"No, she'll tell you. We'll be back," Crosslin said.

Mandy got out of the car and waved to Jill. She was so relieved her friend was there. Running to Jill's side she noticed she carried a pillow. Jill had on matching blue denim jeans, jacket and cap. "Boy, am I glad to see you, Jill. I like your cap," Mandy said.

"Thanks," Jill said. "My grandparents bought it for me."

Mandy noticed Jill seemed paler than usual. "I'm real glad to see you. Did Crosslin tell you how everything went yesterday?"

Jill smiled. "He did and I'm so glad. Mandy, I felt terrible letting you guys down like I did, but I couldn't help it. A lot depended on me, and I had to spend the night and all day at the hospital with my little sister."

"Hospital? What's wrong with her?" Mandy asked.

"Let's sit over here," Jill said. "You need to know the whole story." Jill tossed the pillow she was carrying onto the flat rock near the water. She sat down on the pillow very carefully. "My six-year-old sister woke up one morning running a high fever and was in a lot of pain. My mom and dad are divorced so my mother wrapped Clarie in a blanket and I held her while my mom drove to the hospital."

Mandy listened intently.

"The doctors did tests and we were there all day. The doctor came out and talked to my mother, and she started crying. I knew it was bad to make my mother cry." Jill wiped away tears. "My sister had a big tumor in her stomach, and it was cancer."

"How awful," Mandy said. She could feel the tears filling her own eyes.

"They didn't give mother much hope for my sister to live, but they wanted to try some new treatments. They gave my sister chemo, and it worked."

"Did she lose her hair?" Mandy asked.

"Yes, it all came out. But the nice thing was when it came back in, it was curly," Jill said.

"Did she like the curly hair?" Mandy asked.

"She loved it, but they had to give her more chemo. She lost her hair again, but the cancer was gone."

"That's great," Mandy said.

"We were so happy," Jill said. "It seemed to be a miracle. My sister did real well for a couple of years, and then one morning she woke up really sick. Mother wrapped her in a blanket, and I held her and we rushed to the hospital again. They said she no longer had the lymphoma cancer, but now she had leukemia."

"Oh no," Mandy gasped. "That's awful."

"Yes, it was. I thought my poor mother was going to have a breakdown. This was really hard on our family."

"Your poor little sister," Mandy said. She suddenly thought of her own little sister, Summer, and missed her terribly.

"They said her only hope was a bone marrow transplant. You have to test all the family to see if anyone is a match. They do this with blood work. My dad flew in, but he wasn't a match. My mom was tested, but she wasn't a match either, so they tested me. I was a perfect match."

"Oh Jill, why didn't you tell Crosslin and me?"

"I don't know. It seems so much like a nightmare, I try to pretend it isn't happening. As long as I don't talk about it, I can pretend that everything is all right."

"We could have helped you, Jill. We're your friends."

Jill smiled and wiped her wet cheeks with the tail of her T-shirt. "Thanks. I haven't had any friends since this happened, and I'm a little out of practice at having friends."

Mandy nodded. "So that is where you were when you couldn't come to the canal to call the manatees."

"Yeah. I had to be in the hospital the night before and then all day when they took my bone marrow."

"Did it hurt?"

Jill nodded. "Yeah, it did. They used a long needle to take it from my lower back. I pretended I was at the canal talking to Marie and Tiny Tina and it wasn't so bad. But I do have a problem. It's hard for me to sit down because it's still sore where the needle went in. I brought a pillow from home to sit on."

"Are you sure you're up to this today?" Mandy asked suddenly feeling sorry she had been angry with Jill for not being with them before.

"I have to be. We have to help the boaters care, so they'll slow down and watch out for the manatees, or they'll soon be gone. They'll listen to their children and grandchildren. The marina kids can help us. Children can make a difference you know."

Jill gazed into the water. "I know the manatees hurt when those boat propellers cut into their backs. My little back pain is nothing compared to what the manatees feel. Maybe we can help people to care."

"We will make a difference, Jill. We will," Mandy said, but in her heart she wasn't sure.

Mandy was glad for the extra time with Jill. They talked about their younger sisters and found they were much alike.

"Did Clarie wear cute hats when she was bald?" Mandy asked.

"She did at first. Our aunts gave her lots of hats, but after a while she quit wearing them. She said her best friends were bald because of their chemo. I guess she figured if they could go without a hat, she could, too."

"Did Crosslin tell you about the field trip and the happenings?"

"No, he just said it went okay. You know Crosslin. He doesn't say more than he has to say."

"Well, let me tell you everything that happened." Mandy told Jill every detail of the trip from what was in the picnic basket to Thurston smarting off to Big Bear.

"I hope Thurston doesn't come today. I don't feel like putting up with his meanness," Jill said.

"I doubt that he'll be invited," Mandy said. "No one wants to be around him. Have you seen the manatees since we saw you last?"

Jill shook her head. "This is my first visit since the three of us were together. I need to tell them where I've been. I need to tell them good-bye."

"Good-bye?" Mandy asked. "Are you leaving?"

"No, but the manatees will soon be leaving," Jill said.

"Why?" Mandy asked.

"When the ocean water gets down to 68 degrees the manatees come to the canals because they need the warm water of the power plant to live. Cold water will kill them," Jill explained. "Some people say the water needs to be at least 74 degrees for them to survive. They stay here in the warm water behind the power plant until the ocean water warms up. Then they return home."

"Good grief," Mandy said. "Those poor creatures. They have to worry about the boats and they have to worry about the water getting too cold."

"They probably will leave by the end of March, or if the ocean stays cold, the first part of April. I want to talk to them before they swim away," Jill said.

"Will they come back next year?" Mandy asked.

"Probably, if they are still alive. My grandparents are here to buy a house, so we can live with them," Jill said.

"Oh Jill, that is terrific. I'll come back every chance I can. We can write to each other, and I'll let you know when I'm coming back to Vero Beach."

"Whenever I can, I'll stop by and visit with your grandmother. That way she can tell me when you're coming back," Jill said. "Now, let me call the manatees so I can talk with them before the others gets here."

Jill broke a twig off a bush and brushed it back and forth in the water. She concentrated so hard, willing the manatees to surface, that Mandy was sure Jill had forgotten she was beside her. "Come see me, my beloveds. I've missed you so much. Come see me, my friends," Jill said.

To Mandy's amazement, four faces appeared just above the water. She had never seen the manatees raise their faces so far out of the water. This time Mandy heard squeaks. The sound came from back in the manatees' throats as if they were talking to Jill.

The wind was blowing and tears seemed to be coming down from their eyes. Soon tears were streaming from Jill's eyes. "I'm so glad to see you guys. I was afraid you would be gone. I have so much to tell you."

Mandy listened as Jill told the manatees how sick her sister had been. "I've really missed you guys. You're going to have some visitors, so you be on your best behavior. These kids can help save you." The manatees bobbed their heads as if to say, "Yes, we understand."

Mandy scooted next to Jill to see the manatees closer.

Jill pointed. "Oh look, Mandy, Marie's baby has a mark on her tail. I wonder where she got that?" Jill looked closely. "It doesn't seem to be cut through. I think she'll be all right."

"Do you think it was a boat?"

"Probably and that scares me," Jill said.

"Why?" Mandy asked.

"Because if she is going close to boats that means Marie is going close as well." Jill shook her finger at the manatees.

"You guys stay away from people, and those boats. They will cut you to pieces. Do you hear me? Stay away from them."

The manatees squeaked and squealed as if they had understood what Jill had said.

"Can they hear the boats from under the water?" Mandy asked.

Jill shook her head. "No. My dad is a diver, and he said he could never tell where the boats were coming from when he was under the water. He said the sound seems to be all around. I guess manatees can't tell either, or they would get out of the boat's way."

"That is so sad. That scar on Tiny Tina seems to look like a "Z.""

"Well, she's lucky to still be alive. That boat could have cut her open. At least we'll always know her now by that "Z" on her tail.

Mandy pointed. "Look, Big Bear is coming with the marina kids. You better hurry, and tell the manatees what you want to tell them."

Jill looked at the four gray faces gazing up at her. "Guys, I wanted to tell you where I had been and to tell you to be careful when you leave here. I'll see you next year at this very place. Promise me, you'll come back here to be with me if you're still alive." Jill's voice cracked. "You better find warm places when it is cold and remember to stay away from the boats."

Mandy could see the kids from the marina rushing toward them and waved. She quickly turned to Jill. "It's great that you'll be here when they return next year."

"It would be neat if you could come back again on spring break to help me welcome the manatees back," Jill said.

"I'll try real hard to come back. I'll talk to Nana about it," Mandy said.

The manatees disappeared under the water and could not be seen.

The thundering herd of breathless kids from the marina stopped in front of Mandy and Jill.

"Where are they?" Ruby asked. "Jill, will they really come to you when you signal them?"

Jill nodded. "Yes, they're waiting to meet you guys."

Picking up the crepe myrtle twig, Jill swished the twig in the water and four faces appeared.

"Wow!" the kids said.

"Everyone, I want you to meet Tiny Tina on the left, then her mother, Marie next to her."

Some of the children hurried to the bank where they could see Tiny Tina. "Isn't she cute?" they chimed.

"Are you sure it's a girl?" Big Bear asked and chuckled.

Jill nodded. "It's a girl."

Crosslin's grandfather told them how the manatee mother keeps the baby close to her for at least two years. "The mother doesn't have another baby until that one is ready to be on its own."

"The baby nurses," Rabbit Who Hops said.

"How?" Greg, one of the eight-year-old boys asked.

"From the faucet under her flipper, Stupid," Butch said. "The little baby stays right at her side because that is where the milk is."

Rabbit Who Hops continued, "That is true, but she also teaches her calf what it needs to know to survive."

"Like what?" Ruby's sister, Megan asked.

"Like what plants to eat, and where the water is warm. She also teaches her calf how to return to their home when the ocean is warm, and then when the water gets cold how to return to the warm water places like here in the canal behind the power plant."

"Gosh, that's a lot to learn in two years," Ruby said.

Rabbit Who Hops smiled. "The manatees are like the Indians. Many times they stay together and move to different places together."

Crosslin sat next to his grandfather. "Grandfather, tell them the story that your grandfather told about what his grandfather had seen."

"This is a story my grandfather told me. When the government took away our land and forced us to leave, 500 of our Seminole braves fled into the Florida swamp. They couldn't fish because the water wasn't clear and times became hard for the Seminoles. The mosquitoes were thick. Many Seminoles died. Hunting was difficult because it was like a muddy jungle. It was cold in the winter and hot in the summer. Our people were starving and prayed to the Great Spirit to send help. Within a short time, a manatee appeared and spoke to our people, 'I am here to save you. But in time you must save me.' The manatee had swum away from a faraway herd of manatees and allowed itself to be taken to provide food for the 500 who were starving. They took all the meat from the manatee and the Indian squaws prepared the meat to dry so it would last well into the winter.

"When the sky became dark, they left the skin at the edge of the water. The next morning when they returned for the skin which they would use in many ways they found a baby manatee calf lying upon the skin. It was still alive and was trying to stay close to its mother. The Indians squaws wept and took the baby calf into the water so it would live. Another female manatee swam by and raised its flipper to show the baby its udder. The baby nursed from the other female manatee, and he and his new foster mother joined the large herd of manatees and swam away. My grandfather's people vowed because of that one manatee's sacrifice to never kill a manatee again."

Looking over at Jill, Mandy noticed she was still sitting on her pillow. By then Jill had swished the crepe myrtle twig into the water, and Brutus' huge shadowy figure moved close to Marie and to Jill. "Everyone, this is Brutus," Jill said.

"Why is he so big?" Butch asked.

"Because he is male and he is old," Big Bear said. "He is probably about 12 feet in length and weighs up to 3,500 pounds."

"Wow!" Butch said. "What's that on his back?" Butch seemed more interested in the big manatee than Marie and her baby.

"It's algae," Jill said. "The fish like to eat the algae and the manatees seem to like for them to eat it, too. Sometimes you'll see lots of fish above the manatees and that is what they're doing. They're eating the algae."

Soon another shadowy figure appeared and Mandy knew from how huge the circles were that it was the biggest manatee, Tubs. "Come here, Tubs," Mandy said to no avail.

"Come here, Tubs." As Jill spoke, the manatee swam and stopped in front of her. When he surfaced his back showed. "What's that on his back?" Ruby asked.

"Initials," Mandy said. "A long time ago, some stupid person carved initials into poor Tubs' back."

The children reacted with groans. "Poor Tubs," Ruby said.

"We're sorry, Tubs, that someone hurt you," Megan said.

"If I could find them, I'd punch their lights out," Butch said.

"Now, if they did anything like this they would go to jail," Jill said. "This was done a long time ago. Rabbit Who Hops was there. He mixed herbs and treated the cut so it wouldn't get infected."

"What do the initials say?" Butch asked.

"S. K.," Jill said. "Our manatee friends here need your help. They'll all be killed if the boaters don't go slow and watch for them so they can avoid hitting them. You need to ask your parents and grandparents to please go slowly in and outside the manatee zones. The manatee can't read, and they get outside the marked areas and get so badly cut up by the propeller blades of the boats that they die. There is something that can be put over the propeller blades and perhaps your parents and grandparents could check that out."

Mandy told them what Jill had said. Neither divers nor manatees can tell where the boats are from the sound of the motor, because under the water the sound seems to be all around.

Jill explained how when the ocean water was cold, the manatee have to go to the areas where they can find warm water so they don't die from the cold. "Behind a power plant is one place they like because of the warm water. If the power plant suddenly gets frugal and decides to shut down to save people money on their electric bill, the manatees don't have a warm place to go to stay alive."

"Oh no," Butch said. "They wouldn't do that? Would they?"

"One town did. It didn't make sense to me," Jill said. "The manatees are here just a few months. Surely each town can do its part to help keep them alive. We just have a few left and people need to care."

"Kids, don't let anyone leave any kind of floating plastic in the water. The manatees eat it and it kills them," Big Bear said.

The children watched the manatees for quite a while. The manatees would go under the water and then return like curious children. At last, all the children had learned the names of the manatees there. Jill cautioned the children to only look at the manatees, and not pet them so they wouldn't swim out to people in boats. Mandy felt proud that their plan had worked.

"Now," Big Bear said. "I want to know how many would like to take a ride on my big boat?"

All the children shouted, "We do."

Mandy smiled. Crosslin had told her Big Bear had asked permission from each parent or grandparent.

"Where's Thurston?" Mandy asked. "Jill was worried he would come. She said she didn't feel up to dealing with him."

"He said he didn't want to be with all us stupid people," Crosslin said.

"Well, it's better he didn't come. Do you think we're about ready to go? Did Jill's mother say she could go?"

"No. Jill's mother wants her back at the hospital. She doesn't want her to go out on the boat. She wants her near her little sister."

"I bet she's afraid Jill might be overdoing it," Mandy said. "She looks really tired today."

"You're probably right," Crosslin said. "We better go. Big Bear is loading up the van."

They stopped by the hospital, and Mandy ran in with Jill to meet her mother. Her mother had on a surgical mask and gown and gloves, and was in the enclosed glass room with Jill's little sister so Mandy just waved.

"We have to be careful of germs so Mother stays in there. The doctors gave Clarie massive dosages of chemo and radiation for four days. She doesn't have any resistance so she has to stay in that glass room until her count goes back up. She'll get well after she gets her resistance built up," Jill said.

"It's great that everything is working out for her. Do you want to ask your mother if you can stay a day or two with my grandmother and me? We have twin beds in the guestroom. Grandmother told me it would be fine to ask you."

"Maybe tomorrow night. I need to stay close to Clarie and Mother tonight in case anything goes wrong. Mother gets scared all alone."

"Call me or give me your telephone number here, and I'll call you and tell you about the boat ride."

Jill quickly wrote down the telephone number for Mandy.

Mandy hugged her and left.

Mandy heard the chatter of all the marina kids in the van as she went out the front door of the hospital. She just shook her head and grinned. She knew they were excited about going for the boat ride.

"Hurry up," they shouted.

Mandy giggled.

"How is Jill's little sister?" Crosslin asked.

"I don't know. She was still in that glassed-in room, but she waved. She's real cute, but she doesn't have any hair," Mandy said.

"Why doesn't she have any hair?" Ruby asked.

"She probably has cancer," Butch said. "My uncle had cancer, and he lost his hair."

Big Bear smiled. "I know lots of fellows who lost their hair and they don't have cancer."

Rabbit Who Hops hit Big Bear's shoulder. "I bet they weren't our people. Native American people don't usually lose their hair."

Crosslin seemed curious about the hair issue. "Why don't Indian people lose their hair?" Crosslin asked.

"Maybe the Great Spirit figured if we had to lose our land we shouldn't have to lose our hair," Big Bear said and he and Rabbit Who Hops laughed and laughed and slapped their knees.

Crosslin just shook his head.

Big Bear pulled in front of the marina, and all the kids hurried to his yacht. Big Bear signaled to the captain and the yacht pulled away from the dock.

June, Big Bear's wife, was nearby to greet each child.

"Could we go around toward the canals and see where we were before?" Mandy asked.

"Sure," Big Bear answered and gave instructions to his captain. Soon the big boat swung around and headed toward the canals near the power plant. As soon as they got near the canals, they saw the most awful sight. A boat had stopped and an injured manatee was floating on top of the water.

Mandy felt a chill. She knew the boat had hit a manatee and perhaps killed it. She looked at the other children and they all seemed to sense something terrible was going on. As their big boat neared, they saw the manatee had big cuts along its back. Next to it was a baby calf with a mark on its tail.

Mandy felt the breath go out of her body, but somehow she managed to yell, "It's Marie. They hit Marie, and she's hurt bad." The men in the other two boats didn't seem to know what to do.

Big Bear shouted to his captain, "Get as close as you can so no other boat will hit her again." Crosslin's grandfather, Rabbit Who Hops, dove into the water and swam to Marie's side. He shouted, "Big Bear, radio the rescue group from Sea World. Tell them to hurry. We have one badly injured manatee and one baby. If they are going to save her they'll have to get here plenty quick."

Butch pointed. "That's my grandfather's boat. Did it hit her?"

Mandy watched as another man dove from the other boat.

"That was my grandfather. I bet he hit her," Butch said.

Crosslin's grandfather and Butch's grandfather tried to comfort Marie.

The calf seemed frightened and suddenly disappeared.

"Where did Tiny Tina go?" Mandy asked. "She isn't around Marie?"

Big Bear called to Rabbit Who Hops, "Where is the calf?"

"We don't know," Rabbit Who Hops answered. "She isn't here."

"Oh no," Mandy said. "We need to call Jill. She can help us find Tiny Tina. When they transport Marie to Sea World, they need to take her baby with her or it will die. Can we guide Marie back to the canals?"

"She seems to be in shock," Rabbit Who Hops said. "Throw me a life jacket. I'm getting tired of treading water. Did the captain reach Sea World?"

"They're on their way," Big Bear said, "but maybe we should go back and get Jill so she can find Tiny Tina. That baby needs to stay with her mother."

"May I call Jill at the hospital?" Mandy asked. "My grandmother can pick her up and bring her to the dock so we can take her out to where Marie is. Maybe Jill can guide her to the canals and find her baby."

"My cell phone is still acting up," Big Bear said. "We used the ship to shore radio to get the rescue group. Let me see what we can do." Big Bear soon returned. "We can't get through to that number. We're just a few minutes from the dock. We'll head back there to call Jill. Rabbit Who Hops, do you want to stay with the manatee or go to the dock with us? We're going after Jill to help us find Marie's baby."

"I'll stay with Marie. We've got to find her calf. Get Jill quick," Rabbit Who Hops said as a huge wave washed over him again. He quickly surfaced. "Go, get Jill. I'll be fine," he ordered.

"Just stay out of the shark's mouth, my friend," Big Bear yelled.

"Go, go. I'll be fine," Rabbit Who Hops called.

"Are you kidding about a shark?" Mandy asked.

"Not kidding," Big Bear said. "Last year they had a bad shark attack not far from here. You can bet a shark knows the minute you enter his water."

Just then a huge wave washed over Rabbit Who Hops again and a chill went through Mandy's body. "Crosslin, do you think your grandfather is safe out in the water?"

"Grandfather is unafraid. The other boat is staying near. Knowing Grandfather, he won't leave the injured manatee."

Ruby took Mandy's hand. Megan came over to hold Mandy's other hand.

Mandy couldn't be quiet any longer. "Big Bear, is Marie going to die?" she asked.

"She could. Many do. She'll die without her calf. We've got to find that little one. That baby will give her mother a reason to live."

Mandy felt more hopeful. She wished someone had a cell phone so she could tell Jill what was going on. As she looked around, she saw Thurston on the dock talking on his phone. A phone, at last. They could use his phone and Big Bear's wife could run her to the hospital to pick up Jill.

"Ruby, we need to use Thurston's phone," Mandy said.

"He never lets anyone use his phone," Megan said.

Ruby charged ahead, off the boat and straight to Thurston. "Thurston, we need to borrow your phone for just a minute. It's real important."

Thurston smirked. "You're pretty stupid if you think I'm letting you use my phone."

Ruby grabbed the phone, and she and Mandy ran off the dock with it. "What's the number?" she shouted to Mandy. Mandy read off the number and Ruby punched the numbers and listened. "It's ringing."

Mandy took the phone. Jill answered. They still were running from the walkway to the shore with Thurston right behind them. Mandy panted out of breath, "Jill, we need you at the marina right now. Marie was hit by a boat. She's in shock. Sea World Rescue is on the way, but we can't find Tiny Tina. We're going to have to find her so she can go with her mother."

"My grandparents are here," Jill said. "Grandpa will drive me to the marina. I'll be there in five minutes."

As soon as Mandy saw Thurston approach them she wasn't sure she and Ruby would be alive in five minutes.

Ruby grabbed the phone from Mandy's hand. "It was a local call," Ruby said. "I'll pay you for it."

"You bet you will or I'll have my grandfather bill you."

"You stingy old thing. We had an emergency. One of the manatees was hit by a boat."

"Is it dead?" Thurston asked.

"No, she's still alive," Ruby said. "Sea World Rescue will be here soon."

"Too bad," he said, smirking. "I found the sign I made. I think I'll put it back up on the marina to welcome the kids back."

Thurston pulled the sign from beneath the barrel where they had hidden it. "I saw Jill cry. I saw you guys put the sign here the other day. The sign seemed to upset Jill. I think I'll put it back up to upset her a little more."

Mandy didn't know what came over her, but she'd had enough of this mean spirited brat named Thurston. "You dumb jerk. Jill's little sister is in the hospital fighting cancer. I don't think she needs to be upset any more than she is. She loves every one of those manatees, and now one is hurt real bad. If you put that sign up I think all of us in the Manatee Club will take care of you. Do you understand what I'm saying?"

"You don't scare me?" Thurston sneered. "Girls can't fight."

"No, but boys can," Butch said and pushed Thurston down to his knees. "And while you're there you might say a prayer for Marie because my grandfather's boat hit her and he's pretty upset."

"I'm going home," Thurston said. "I don't want to be around all you stupids."

"The only stupid person here is you, Thurston," Ruby said. "Stay off of my dad's marina. You're not welcome any more. If I ever see that sign anywhere around, I'll call the police."

When Mandy looked up, Jill and her grandfather were hurrying toward her on the walkway.

"If you need a ride back to the hospital, call me," he called as he turned and headed back to his car.

Mandy ran to meet Jill. "This way," she shouted. They ran across the gangplank onto the yacht. Big Bear signaled to the captain and the boat pulled away from the dock. They were soon out in the water where Crosslin's grandfather and Marie were. Butch's grandfather's boat was smaller than Big Bear's yacht but it was a beautiful boat. It was anchored next to Marie to protect the manatee from being hit again by another boat.

"Did Tiny Tina come back?" Mandy asked.

"Nope," Rabbit Who Hops said. "She's nowhere in sight. I swam under water all around trying to spot her, but she must have gotten frightened and left. No telling where she is."

Jill was already in the water. Mandy wasn't sure how she had gotten in because she hadn't even heard a splash. She was stroking Marie and talking to her in a calm way. "She's shuddering," Jill said. "She could be in shock. Those cuts are real deep. I hope they hurry. Marie, you hold on. They'll fix you back up. You'll go to a real nice place until you're well and then you get to come back here. Where is your baby? We need to find her so she can go with you to get well. Where is she?"

Mandy heard a squeak from Marie.

Jill cooed and stroked Marie until the manatee seemed calm.

"I think I know where she is," Jill said. "She'll be behind the power plant with the other manatees. Big Bear, may we take the dinghy and paddle to the canals to look for her? The water is calm. We can look for circles."

"Good idea. It's a short distance. Raise the paddle if you find her or need help."

"She'll be coming up for air soon," Jill said.

"How do you know?" Mandy asked.

"They usually come up every five to 20 minutes," Jill called from the water. "Untie the dinghy and give us life jackets and we'll be fine."

Mandy's heart raced as they untied the small boat. She couldn't believe she was going to do this with Jill. Jill swam like a mermaid. She swam, but she hated to get her face in the water. Even in the shower she hated for the water to run down her face. Sure, she could save herself, but what was she getting into?

Jill seemed to realize Mandy's mood. "Are you okay?"

"I don't swim under water very well," she said.

"Well, just put the life jacket on. I swim well enough for both of us."

Mandy quickly put the life jacket on and soon the two were in the small boat and headed for the canals. Mandy said, "I didn't tell you everything."

"Everything, what?" Jill asked.

"I said I don't swim under water very well. Well, I lied. I don't swim under water at all. I hate to get water up my nose."

"Well, can you row?" Jill asked.

"Yeah, I can do that," Mandy said and giggled nervously.

"Well, you row, and I'll look for circles from the baby," Jill said.

Mandy was amazed at how confident Jill was. They arrived at the canals and Jill took her life jacket off and got in the water. She swam under water looking for the baby. Soon all the other manatees were gathering around the boat.

"If the baby were here, I feel it would be with the other manatees. But it isn't. No telling where she went."

Tubs seemed to be nudging Jill toward the shore. "What are you trying to tell me, Tubs?" Jill asked.

"Go where he wants you to go," Mandy said.

"I think I will. He's acting like he knows something." Jill dove under the water and came back up. "There's a pipe down there and I think Tiny Tina is frightened and hiding in it. I'll try to pull her out if I can." Jill came up gasping for air. "I can't get her. Let me try again." Jill dove under the water and again came back up gasping, "I can't do it by myself. You have to help me."

Mandy's heart pounded. "Did I tell you swimming under water isn't my thing?" she asked.

"What are we going to do then?" Jill answered.

"I'm going to hold up the paddle and get help," Mandy said.

"There isn't time. She hasn't been up for air for a long time, and she's going to die if we don't get her out now."

"I give up. What do you want me to do?" Mandy asked.

"You'll have to take off your life jacket so you can dive under water and I'll hold your hand and you can hold your breath, and we'll pull as hard as we can."

Mandy felt her heart pounding as she removed her life jacket. "Lord, help me," she prayed. "Jill, don't let go of my hand."

"I won't until we get to the pipe. Take hold of the pipe with your left hand and reach in and pull hard with the right hand, and I'll be pulling, too. We'll get her unstuck, and we'll head for the surface with her. You hold onto the back of my shirt."

It sounded easier than it was. They got to the pipe and Mandy took hold of the pipe with her left hand and tried to get hold of the baby manatee, but she was shaking so hard she couldn't reach in without letting go of her left hand. Soon she was out of air and motioned to Jill to go up.

Mandy hung so tightly to the back of Jill's shirt she almost pulled it off. They surfaced and clung to the side of the boat to catch their breath.

"I couldn't reach her," Mandy lied. The manatee was on her side of the large pipe. She could have reached her if she had let go of her left hand to reach farther into the pipe. She hadn't because she was afraid.

"I saw a long rope in the boat. I'll tie it to the boat and you can hang on to the rope, and you'll feel safer," Jill said.

Mandy nodded. Before, she could have almost touched the baby manatee. Maybe the rope would give her courage to reach in the pipe farther. "We'll get her this time," Mandy said. "Let's go." Mandy hoped Jill couldn't hear her heart pounding so loudly. Holding the rope in one hand and holding to Jill's shirt with the other, they got back to the pipe.

Mandy reached into the pipe and clenched her teeth as she tugged on Tiny Tina's tail. Jill got her hand into the pipe on the other side, and they both tugged at the same time and Tiny Tina came loose. Mandy let Jill back out the baby manatee and get hold of her.

Hanging onto the rope, Mandy grabbed the back of Jill's shirt, and they headed for the surface and to the small boat. When Mandy grabbed the side of the boat, she spotted her life jacket, and grabbed it out of the boat. She put it on, one arm at a time, so she wouldn't have to let go of the side of the boat. She zipped up the life jacket with one hand.

"Mandy, once Tiny Tina has some air, then we can rest a minute. I'll swim with her out to Marie. Can you get into the little boat?"

"Nope, but I can reach the paddle and hold it up so they'll come and help us."

Mandy reached the oar and held it up. "I hope they see this," Mandy said.

"They did. They're coming this way," Jill said.

Soon, Big Bear was in the water helping Mandy get to the ladder of the yacht. When she got on board she was never so glad to be anywhere in her life.

By then, Jill had Tiny Tina by Marie's side. Marie seemed to calm as soon as she saw her baby.

"Look," Mandy said. "There's a rescue boat. They're here and they can take both Marie and Tiny Tina with them. They'll make her well. I just know they will."

Big Bear got into the water to help Jill get onto the yacht.

Soon, there were divers in the water with equipment to get Marie to the closest dock to load her into the large truck.

"This is a serious injury," one diver said. "We'll do what we can." Soon, the workers had the baby and Marie in the truck together and they sped away to Sea World.

"They'll keep the manatees wet until they get to Sea World, and they'll treat Marie's injuries and put them in a large tank."

"I hope Marie will live," Jill said.

"She'll live. She has her baby to live for thanks to you, Jill," Mandy said.

"Well, thanks to you, too. I couldn't get her pulled out alone. You helped pull her out. I want you to promise me that this year when you go back home, you'll learn how to swim under water. You'll get used to having water in your face. Everyone needs to know how to swim both ways," Jill said.

"I promise. Next spring break, I intend to swim like a fish or a mermaid like you."

"Or a manatee. Did you know they used to think the manatees were mermaids?"

"Good grief. They would be ugly mermaids," Mandy said.

"I know," Jill said and giggled.

Mandy looked around the boat. Crosslin's grandfather was exhausted. His long braids dripped with water. Butch's grandfather was sitting next to him. His hair was pushed to one side and on his right temple was a large scar. Mandy looked around the boat for Crosslin. She motioned for him to come to her side. "Did you see Butch's grandfather's scar?"

"No," Crosslin said.

"Do you think your grandfather saw his scar?" Mandy asked.

"Grandfather misses nothing. I believe he saw the scar and knows exactly who that fellow is and what he did in the past."

"Your grandfather said he would wear his shame like a blanket. He sure stayed down in that water a long time to try to comfort Marie. Let's tell Jill what we think," Mandy said.

Soon everyone was wrapped in towels and Crosslin's grandfather said, "Mr. Smart Kid here wants to tell you something."

Butch looked puzzled. He whispered to Mandy, "Why is he saying that?"

Mandy knew what was coming. "Just listen," she said.

Everyone got quiet. "When I was young like you, I did something that I've been ashamed about all my life. I had a friend who was mean and liked to do mean things. You probably know his grandson, Thurston."

All of the kids nodded.

"Well, he had a new knife and I thought it was a pretty keen knife. He said he would give me the knife if I would do what he told me to do. Well, I wanted that knife in the worst way. There was a manatee that stayed under the dock most of the time. He said, 'Carve S. K. for smart kid on the back of that manatee and you can have the knife.'

"I did it and Rabbit Who Hops saw me. He was just a young fellow. He picked up a rock and knocked me backwards, and I had a hole in my forehead to remind me every day of the shameful thing I did. I want to tell you how that affected me my entire life. Every day when I parted and combed my hair, I remembered. Whenever I would hear about the manatees dying, I remembered. Everything reminded me of my shame."

No one said a word.

"I want to say to Jill, to the manatees, and to all of you how sorry I am. I want to warn you not to let other people persuade you to do anything which is bad and shameful. I got in the water with the injured manatee to tell her how sorry I was. I didn't hit her. A speedboat hit her, but I saw what happened and I stopped to help. I want to ask Rabbit Who Hops to forgive me and especially my grandson, Butch, and Jill and all of you who love the manatees. Please say you forgive me."

"We forgive you," they all said together.

The old man put his head in his hands and wept. All the children encircled him and patted his shoulder. No one said a word.

Rabbit Who Hops walked over to the man and put his hand on the man's shoulder. "Now, it is time to forgive yourself."

Mandy couldn't help it. The tears flowed. She had felt like crying when her grandmother had told her the story of the Trail of Tears, but she had held the tears back. Then she held back the tears when she saw poor Marie with the chunk cut out of her back. But to see this poor old man crying over what he had done many years before was more than she could stand. She felt the sobs come, and she cried until she was empty. When she looked around, all the other children were crying, too.

When Mandy got home, she told her grandmother about everything that had happened and asked if Jill could stay with them. "Nana, her grandparents had to leave. She'll have to stay at home alone or just sit at that hospital. That's no fun. Could we ask her? Please, please."

Her grandmother agreed. They called the hospital and spoke to Jill's mother. Jill's sister was doing well so arrangements were made for Jill to spend the next few nights with Mandy.

The next day Big Bear took the marina children, Jill, Crosslin and Mandy back to the canals for them to be with the manatees. By then all the children knew all the manatees' names and you could tell the children considered the manatees their personal friends. They vowed to teach their parents and grandparents to slow down and watch for the manatees. Now, there were lots of members of their own little manatee group and they were going to join the Save the Manatee Club and check on adopting a manatee. Things were better than Mandy had ever hoped.

Saturday was their last full day together. Mandy and Jill played in the ocean, and walked the beach to pick up shells for Mandy to take back home.

When they got back to her grandmother's house, they taught Jill how to send e-mails on the computer. She could now send an e-mail to Mandy when Mandy returned to Oklahoma, and they could keep in touch. Big Bear had arranged for the person in charge of Marie's care to e-mail her progress to Jill in care of Mandy's grandmother. Her grandmother could forward the e-mail on to Mandy in Oklahoma. Thus far, Marie was still alive and doing well.

"I'll take you girls to the beach at first light," her grandmother said.

"First light? What is that Nana?" Mandy asked.

Grandmother smiled. "It's when the sun first comes up and you can barely see. If we're there first, we can make the first footprints in the sand."

"That sounds like fun. Doesn't it, Jill?" Mandy asked.

"Yeah, it does. I've never done that before," Jill replied.

"Nana, can we get up while it is still dark so we can make sure we're the first one on the beach?" Mandy asked.

Her grandmother smiled. "I'll set the alarm."

"When does Mandy have to leave?" Jill asked.

"We have to allow an hour and a half to get to the Melbourne airport. You need to be at the airport an hour early so we'll have to leave by 11:20 a.m."

"Nana, I sure hate to leave. I wish I lived with you all the time."

"I wish you did, too, but we'll manage to get you here more often. I promise." She hurried out of the room.

Mandy gathered up her clothes to put in the suitcase. "I'll wear these jeans and top on the plane," she said as she draped them over the back of a chair.

Jill sat on one of the twin beds. "I wish you could stay longer."

Mandy sat on the other bed facing Jill. She hated to leave Vero Beach and her new found friends. Jill and Crosslin were so important to her now. "I dread leaving. Mom said they just had a six-inch snow. She'll bring my heavy coat to the airport."

Mandy went to the closet and looked and then pulled out the drawer of the dresser. She called to her grandmother, "Nana, I'm missing some of my clothes." She turned to Jill. "Not like I'll need shorts to play in the snow. I'll probably be able to wear my Florida clothes in June in Oklahoma."

"I have your missing clothes right here," her grandmother said. "I didn't want to send any dirty laundry home with you. Your mother is busy enough working and caring for Summer. I wish I lived closer so I could help her more."

"Me, too," Mandy said. "Nana, what did we do with all those little shells with the hole in the top. I want to share those with my track team. They can put a thin ribbon or chain through them for a necklace."

"I washed the sand off them, and they're on a towel on the kitchen cabinet," her grandmother said.

On the beach she and Jill had taken plastic sacks to pick up shells. The white ones with the hole in the top had been her favorite.

Jill locked her arms in front of her. "Next year I'll show you how to find sand dollars in the water. They're hard to find because they are dark colored. You have to clean them, and then they're white," Jill said.

"That will be fun," Mandy said.

Grandmother folded the clothes and handed them to Mandy to put in her suitcase. "I have a bag of oranges for you to take back. I ran to the grove and got them," she said.

"Will they let me take them on the plane?" Mandy asked.

Grandmother nodded. "Yes, they check them with your luggage. Everyone takes oranges back. I even found some Honeybells. They are sweet as sugar and usually all gone by now but one grove had some left. We'll have them put in a box so they don't get mashed."

Mandy hugged her grandmother. "Nana, I have had the best time thanks to you and Jill."

"How about Crosslin, Fawn, Big Bear and Rabbit Who Hops?" Jill asked.

"Well, thanks to them, too. I wouldn't have been here if it hadn't been for Nana sending me the airline ticket. Mother could never afford it," Mandy said.

"Well, you can come as often as you're able. I'll manage the fare some way."

"Do you have your Dream Catcher packed?"

"No, I'll take it off the wall in the morning. I don't want to have nightmares tonight," Mandy said.

Soon, the phone rang and Grandmother called to Mandy. "It's your mother. She wants to make sure you're coming home."

Mandy giggled. "I wish I could say I was staying but that would hurt her feelings." Taking the phone she said, "Hi, Mom. See you tomorrow. Be sure and bring Summer. I have her a dream catcher for a present. Don't tell her. Don't forget my coat. Love you." She hung up.

Grandmother smiled. "I spoke to your mother earlier. She said she has had a lot of depression this past year. She said she has decided to go to a support group."

Mandy looked down at the floor. "I thought it was my fault that she was so unhappy and slept so much."

"I was afraid of that," her grandmother said. "Your mother mentioned you seemed to blame yourself for your dad's death."

Mandy felt a shiver go through her body. "I didn't want you to find out."

"Find out what, Mandy?"

"Find out that it was my fault Daddy died. If I had gone to run with him, I could have called 911. I could have saved him. I didn't go and he died. Grandmother, please don't hate me."

Grandmother enfolded Mandy into her arms. Shaking her head her grandmother said, "First, you need to know the truth. It wasn't your fault. Your dad was born with a heart defect. The doctors told him he wouldn't live to finish high school."

"Oh, Nana," Mandy gasped.

Grandmother continued, "He fell in love and married your mother. He never told her. It wasn't fair to her. It was no one's fault. You would have gone with him if you had known. Perhaps it was his fault for not telling, but he felt God had been good to him to give him so many years and such a wonderful family. He was very proud of you. You couldn't have saved him if you had been with him."

Tears streamed down Mandy's face. "He died alone. No one should die alone."

"No, he didn't die alone. His grandfather and grandmother were there with him to help him. Now he's in heaven with them, and his heart is now perfect. He worries about your mother and you feeling such guilt. He wants you to get over that. Can you?"

Mandy looked up into her grandmother's eyes. "Is he okay up in heaven?"

"He will be as soon as you and your mother get well and happy again."

"I'll try. I want to be happy again. I used to be happy all the time."

"I remember," Grandmother said. "You always woke up smiling."

Jill hugged Mandy. "I felt guilty, too, that I was well and my baby sister was almost dying. Somehow it didn't seem fair."

Grandmother smiled. "Things are going to be better for everyone now. I just know it."

"I know it, too, but I need to call the hospital." Jill called her mother to make sure her sister was still fine. She was.

"Let's go tell Crosslin and Fawn and Rabbit Who Hops good-bye," Mandy said. When they rang the doorbell there was no answer. "Oh pooh, there is no one home," Mandy said.

"Let's go feed the gulls before it gets too late," Jill said.

They ran to the kitchen to get the stale bread from the refrigerator. Grandmother kept it there so it wouldn't mold.

"Nana," Mandy called to her grandmother, "We're going to feed the gulls. Okay?"

"Okay," her grandmother called back.

They hurried to the boardwalk to toss bread to the gulls. A lady feeding the gulls beside them told them she had tossed a hunk of bread and her diamond ring flew off. A gull caught the ring, swallowed it, and flew away.

"Oh no," Mandy said. "That's terrible."

"Yes, it was," the lady said, "but it was insured."

They all laughed about the ring.

They looked out at the ocean and watched the children dig in the sand. Mandy looked at Jill. "I'm getting hungry. Are you?"

"Sorta," Jill said.

Grandmother looked up when the screen door popped as they walked into the house. "Do you girls like hamburgers?"

"Yes," they chimed. Soon, they were going through a drive-through for hamburgers and french fries. They ate in the car. When they got home, they showered and got ready for bed.

The next morning, Mandy heard the alarm go off. Jill was sleeping soundly. "Jill, wake up. I heard the alarm."

"Is it morning already? I feel like I just went to sleep," Jill said.

They were dressed by the time Grandmother came down the hall. Mandy took the Dream Catcher off the wall and put it in her suitcase with Summer's Dream Catcher and a mesh bag of orange flavored gum they had bought at the grove. The three of them walked to the beach. Nana took a flashlight because it was barely light. The sun looked like a giant orange as it rose over the ocean.

As Mandy and Jill pulled off their socks, she said, "Nana, take a picture of the sun. It's so beautiful." Grandmother took the photo and then pulled off her sandals. "Okay, girls, let's make the first prints in the sand. "Mandy, you get in the middle." They ran down the beach holding hands and Mandy knew she would never forget this special morning.

When they returned home, Mandy showered and dressed and she, Jill and Grandmother ate hot cakes and bacon for breakfast.

"I hope Crosslin is home so I can talk to him before I leave," Mandy said.

"Let's go see," Jill said.

They ran next door and knocked on the door. No one answered.

Jill shaded her eyes and peeked in the front window. "They aren't home."

Mandy fought down the sadness. How could she leave and not even tell Crosslin good-bye? Someone had said when you wake up you can choose happy or sad and from now on she was going to choose happy. "I'm kinda disappointed I don't get to tell Crosslin good-bye. I guess I can send him an e-mail and Nana can print it out and give it to him."

"That's about all you can do if he isn't home," Jill said. "I got the feeling he was a little sweet on you," she teased.

"Pooh, I got the feeling he had a crush on you," Mandy said.

"That's a joke. I see how he looks at you, Mandy. He likes you."

"Sure, as a friend but not as a boyfriend."

"Want to bet?" Jill asked.

"No," Mandy said. "But he helped me have the best vacation ever."

"Well, maybe he'll get home before we leave for the airport," Jill said.

Mandy kept going to the window to see if Crosslin had returned, but there was still no one home.

Grandmother looked at her watch. "We better load up the car. I don't want to have to hurry. They look for speeders in the little towns on the way to Melbourne."

As they pulled out of the driveway, Mandy looked out the back window to make sure Crosslin hadn't returned. Still no Crosslin. She felt sad that she didn't even get to tell him good-bye.

When they got to the airport, they stood in line for the airport personnel to check the contents of her luggage. Mandy then waited in another line to check in. Grandmother asked the airport personnel to put the oranges in a cardboard fruit box, which they did. Mandy looked at the clock. They were early.

"Better early, than late," her grandmother said. "We'll sit here until it's time to board. Jill and I aren't allowed to go through the metal detectors with you. I don't want you waiting alone."

Mandy was glad. She didn't want to walk up that long aisle and sit by herself as she had done in Atlanta. "Nana, look at the monitors for Atlanta. See if the flight is on time. I'll fly to Atlanta and change planes and fly on into Tulsa."

Grandmother pointed. "On time, it says."

Jill poked Mandy in the shoulder. "Does that scare you having to fly alone?"

Mandy grinned. "Nope, I don't think I'll be afraid of anything after what we went through."

"Right," Jill said.

It was hard leaving. Sure, she missed her mother and Summer, but she felt torn apart having to leave this beautiful place. She had made good friends that she might never see again. Why hadn't she taken time to tell them all how much they meant to her? Why hadn't she started earlier and told each one how much their friendship meant?

When Mandy looked up, she couldn't believe her eyes. Big Bear, Crosslin, Fawn and Rabbit Who Hops walked toward her.

Mandy cried with joy. She finally managed to get the words out, "I'm so glad to see you guys."

"We couldn't let you fly away without telling you good-bye," Big Bear said.

Mandy hugged each one and shared how much they had meant to her. When she finished, she looked at her grandmother. "Nana, thank you so much for letting me come. This was the best vacation of my life."

Her grandmother handed her an envelope. "One of many," she said.

Mandy wasn't sure what that meant until she opened the envelope. Inside was an invitation to return to Vero Beach for the next spring break. It read, "The ticket will be paid for in your name, and you'll pick it up at the airport in Tulsa, Oklahoma. I'll be waiting for you."

"You are brave girl to help the manatee," Big Bear said.

"It took us all to help the manatees," she said. She hugged each one again. When she hugged Crosslin, he pulled something from a plastic sack. He handed her a long stemmed red rose and kissed her on the cheek. "Something to remember me by," he said and blushed.

Jill kissed her on the other cheek and whispered, "See, I told you."

Mandy giggled.

"Thank you, Crosslin. It's beautiful."

Crosslin grinned and looked down.

She hugged her grandmother. "I love you." She reached in her pocket and showed her the rose rock. "Nana, I will always remember."

After saying her good-byes, Mandy boarded the plane. She had the window seat.

As the plane circled over Indian River, the pilot's voice came over the intercom. "If you'll look out your window, you'll see the manatees migrating back out to sea. They visit the canals behind the power plants in Vero Beach because the water is warm. Now they are returning home."

Mandy looked down and saw the manatees in the water. She whispered, "Good-bye, Tubs, good-bye Brutus. Stay safe and I'll see you next year at the canals. Marie and Tiny Tina, I'll see you this summer at Sea World."

She felt tears fill her eyes and reached in her pocket for a tissue. Mandy felt the rose rock and squeezed it tightly. She whispered to herself, "Be safe my precious friends because you are like my people - strong and beautiful and almost gone."

THE END

If your classroom would like more information about saving the manatees or adopting a manatee, write the Save the Manatee Club at the address below:

Save the Manatee Club
500 North Maitland Avenue
Maitland, Florida 32751
1 800-432JOIN (5646)

Call 1-888-404-FWCC to report manatee injuries, deaths, tag sightings, or harassment.

About the Author

Doris Wheelus lives in Sand Springs, Oklahoma. She winters in Vero Beach, Florida. After being introduced to the manatees by a magical little girl at the canals, she dedicated eight years to writing this book hoping to help the endangered gentle giants.

Manatee Girl manuscript won a coveted first place at the state writers contest in Oklahoma City in 2005 in Middle Reader Book. In May, 2006, her Wind Chasers won First Honorable Mention for Best Book in Oklahoma published in 2005.

She has devoted her life to children - teaching them and writing for them.

A loving family of husband, daughter, grandchildren and great-grandchildren surrounds Doris.

Printed in the United States
73159LV00004B/43-84